SCORPION'S TAIL

SCORPION'S
TAIL

G. STAN JONES

atmosphere press

atmospherepress.com

PROLOGUE

The skies darkened to the royal blue of dusk above the foothills of the Sierra Madre when Lomas reached the door of his mud-bricked casucha. It was dinner time and the children of the barrio had untangled from stickball and games of tag on the rutted dirt paths that on the city map of Durango, Mexico, had street names to suggest escape routes from the poorest barrio in the city; from the mud and thatch and adobe walls scattered like weeds on the hard scrabble plain. Calle Rubio, the city map's name for the rut nearest Lomas' home, was many things to its people; a thousand paces to the grist mill, a slippery creek in the rainy season, even a place for meeting or romance but rarely a starting point for another destination.

As the sun's steady crawl above blanketed the front of the tiny house in shadow, Lomas swatted the dust on his T-shirt and jeans and stamped his sandaled feet. The dark-skinned five-year-old seemed swallowed by the shade. His mother wondered how the smallish youngster could have such an appetite. Lomas' belly rumbled as he pushed firmly against the wooden door and just as quickly his eyes froze on his mother, Rosa Ramon Segovia, sprawled on a floor mat in a corner of the one-room hut, dress hiked to the waist and face taut from pain. Before the door bottom had scraped fully open against the hardened caliche floor, her head snapped toward him. Lomas caught only a glimpse of her in the kerosene glow before she screamed at him to leave.

"Out," she stammered in Spanish. "Go outside, Lomas. Now!"

He pulled the door shut with a whoosh and stared at it blankly. Never had his mother spoken to him so and as he stood in the dirt of the lifeless yard, tears filled his eyes. Strange noises were coming from inside, but Lomas dared not try to enter again.

Legs splayed and bent; Rosa braced her head against the mud-thatched wall. When the contractions allowed, she opened her eyes to somehow gauge the progress of the horrible pain wanting out. She made guttural noises that paced the pushing and stretching of labor, subsiding for a time but then rising like a surge of electric current. Air spewed from her lungs in quick breaths as her labor heightened and the baby's head pressed insistently against the mouth of her vagina. Rosa was feeling the worst pain of delivery then, when it seemed she would split in two. She thought of the midwife who hadn't come. She would have clawed at her hand in the rawness of the moment. She scratched at the cool floor instead, frantic, no longer able to speak or scream. Sweat beaded on her forehead as she held her breath and pushed with all her might. Then air gushed from her lungs as the head emerged. She reached down, guided the baby's shoulders while bracing the head and with a final push, Ruben Segovia entered the world. Rosa swatted his bottom until he took his first breath;

when it was over, she placed him on her breast and cried in his hair.

He was with Rosa two days until midwife Teresa Cortez arrived, finally, and claimed him.

CHAPTER 1

2002

In the warm light of her favorite place, the kitchen, Juanita gently stirred a pitcher of margaritas with a wooden spoon. A portable radio pulsed Mexican pop music. Bobbing her head from side to side, she mouthed the words she knew, which weren't many. Music and margaritas were new amusements.

Dressed in a simple shift and T-shirt, she poured her first drink. She swirled the ice with her index finger and sipped. The salt rim made her pucker and lick her lips. She drained the rest in gulps, poured another and began to sway her hips and scoot barefoot along the terrazzo floor. The cool stone felt good but not as good as the margarita was making her feel and she didn't notice the ice shard on the floor until a foot was over it and sliding suddenly out from under her.

With her free hand, she grasped the edge of the island for balance but her drink in the other sloshed over the sides of her glass onto her lap. "Eeeiii," she exclaimed, laughing aloud and steading herself. She grabbed a dish towel from the sink and mopped up with her feet, in the fashion of a dancer tracing the steps of a waltz.

In her room at the back of the ranch style house, she tossed the shift onto the closet floor and chose another with flowers embroidered on it. Folding it over one arm she surveyed her meager wardrobe. A flowing blue dress with a sash for a belt and puffy sleeves caught her eye. She tried to remember ever wearing it. "No," she said, frowning. "Where would I have gone in this? Nowhere. That's where."

She tried it on, and it fit. Standing before her bathroom mirror, Juanita tied the sash behind her back and watched the dress come alive as she spun herself around. But the spinning made her dizzy and with a last glance in the mirror, she slid it off her shoulders and placed it on a hanger. "Another time," she said.

Instead of redressing, she strolled back to the mirror in her underwear. She tied her hair in back and leaned in. She dug in her makeup bag, found the mascara and, pursing her lips to concentrate, lightly coated her eyelashes. Then she powdered her face and added rouge to her cheeks. She stepped back, looked at herself and smiled. Though she'd overdone the rouge, she was pleased. Her body, too, she thought, was pleasant enough for a woman of forty-six, more toned than most of the barrio mothers she'd met, and her skin was unblemished. Her back and shoulders were straight, despite the bending and slouching of endless rounds of house chores.

"You might be a catch!" she said. But she scolded herself for thinking like that.

She was supposed to be in mourning after all. The coroner had measured and sewed the bullet hole shut, concluded the autopsy, and released the body that the funeral home director brought in a Cadillac hearse along with two grave diggers the day before. They dug between two lime trees on the east side of the enclosed yard and eased the pine box with her remains into the earth. A man who confessed to killing Juanita's mother was in jail.

When the funeral director offered to say a few words, Juanita waved him off with a grunt of annoyance. She paid him in cash and the workers filled in the hole and were gone.

Fresh margarita in hand, she opened the heavy front door and closed it gently behind her. The sun was over the house and warm, contrasted by the cool grass on her feet beyond the porch. In a moment she stood over the mound of reddish dirt, took a sip, and pondered how the headstone she'd ordered would look. Some flowers from the courtyard might be nice, she thought.

"A toast!" she said then. "I'm discovering margaritas. It fills the time. Fertilize the lime trees for me, would you? I think you owe me that, Teresa Cortez."

She took a sip and turned away.

CHAPTER 2

1974 - A CALLING

In the early months of 1974, Edwin Youngblood came to believe God finally had taken notice of him. Big things were afoot as if He aimed a divining rod, giving Edwin clarity of purpose as a tuning fork divines the pitch of a violin. He'd been chosen by the Mormon Church to lead a mission to Durango, Mexico, and as its bishop make music from the pulpit.

Edwin wasn't so naïve to believe he was divinely suited for the job. Middle grade Mormon church leaders are neither paid nor deified and are called to serve only after mastering the workings of the business world, as bankers, brokers, or butchers. Edwin was an insurance agent with a kind face and easy smile, and clients in Provo, Utah perceived him as trustworthy. He and his wife, Gabby, were ten years into the business and making good money when the call came. The church ward where they devoted their free hours as elders threw a bash in their honor at the ward hall. All agreed God had singled out Edwin Youngblood for something grand.

If he scrimped and Gabby stayed behind to run things, Edwin could pay his own way to Durango for the three-year mission. Three things bolstered his confidence: He spoke fluent Spanish, having minored in the language at Brigham Young University then honed it daily during eighteen months as a Mormon missionary in Mexico City following graduation; he was a gifted orator with a naturally deep voice and oozy cadence; and he was smart enough to know life can be hard and one should answer the knock of opportunity.

Life before 1974 was hard enough. A promising college football career at Brigham Young died in surgery with a torn knee ligament; he was told his sperm lacked the stamina to bless his household with children; prayers big and small went unanswered but he and Gabby kept the faith as Mormons do.

Durango was to change that.

On the plane ride to El Paso, Edwin prayed for safe passage as lightning below sprayed the spring storm clouds with vein-like bursts. The clouds scraped the mountaintops of Big Bend and belched cool rain on the parched West Texas soil while the pilot eased the aircraft around the worst of it and descended in time to beat the storm to El Paso. An hour later, Edwin crossed the Rio Grande into Mexico by taxi and boarded a bus for Durango. It was a nine-hour trip, but the roads were slick for the first fifty or so miles. As the bus barreled into the Mexican desert and the sun settled behind the mountains, he relaxed his grip on the arm rests.

Out the window, sage, mesquite, and cactus flowers barely moved in the breeze above the reddish dirt as if frozen in time by a watercolor brush. They dotted the landscape for miles before the darkening horizon blurred everything to deep purple. Edwin thought of his first time in Mexico, pedaling a bicycle through the narrow streets of the nation's sprawling capital. It was a luckless place, hunkered down with hands tucked in pockets; a place where even the beggars didn't dare extend their hands without offering something in return; so, they washed windshields with dirty rags at traffic lights or hawked trinkets for pesos worth less than American pocket change. The air was thick with exhaust smoke trapped by the smog, so it hovered above until the rains sent it back down to cover the cars and pavement with a depressing coat of gray.

Edwin felt he was always pedaling uphill there. He sought Mormon converts from among a chronically poor and universally Catholic population. In white shirts, ties, and khaki shorts, going door to door armed with smiles and youthful optimism, Edwin and his fellow missionary were as welcome as marauding banditos. In summer, Edwin's clothes were sweat soaked by mid-morning with an even hotter afternoon to ride out, of slamming doors and oft threatening words. But as his travels led him to outlying barrios and even red-light districts, Edwin found converts in desperately poor day laborers who resented Catholic ritualism. In hovels populated by day with the lonely hearted, Edwin promised salvation without pretense, pointing out that Mormon leaders wore no robes and had day jobs and families. There were those who listened, and a handful followed him to church.

In the end, Edwin found the whole experience bracing like aftershave on razor cuts. Returning to Gabby and Utah, he declared he'd found his calling.

A smile creased Edwin face and he eased lower in his bus seat. The calling was at hand. As the bus wheels whined against the darkness, he rested his eyes and when they blinked open, he was there.

Chapter 3

A Baby's Cry

The Mormon Church's Monterrey mission, established four years prior, was Edwin's blueprint in Durango. An old school building on the fringes of downtown was leased as a temporary ward hall, with half a dozen classrooms, offices, and a cafeteria for Sunday services. Completion of the real mission, planned for Calle Delores Del Rio close to the city center, was two years away. Pockets of Mormons who'd fled anti-polygamy laws in the U.S. were scattered to the north and east of Durango and became Edwin's early targets. He invited them to join the fledgling ward and seated some as elders.

Among them: A barrel-chested former Tennessean with close-cropped red hair and a face exploding with freckles. Ambling in for services one Sunday in a cowboy shirt and jeans, Sterling C. Pierce flashed a gap-toothed grin at Edwin and the elders. When the service ended Sterling slipped quietly out but was back the following week and rarely missed a service after that.

He joked in his thick Southern accent that "life's better

with God on your side. I been there when he wadn't."

He never let on if he was atoning for past transgressions; he'd just smile big and wide, crinkling his freckles into half-moons. "I'm a country boy, just gettin' by," he said to anyone lending an ear. "I've done things, I surely have, but that's in the rearview mirror."

The bishop was still settling in his office in the smaller wing of the flint-colored school when Sterling strode in in a sweat-stained hat and dusty work boots and made quick work of cozying up. "Howdy Bishop. Name's Sterling. Sterling Carat Pierce. Pleased ta know ya."

Edwin gave Sterling an amused shrug. "Let me guess," he asked. "Alabama?"

"Dern close," Sterling said. "Humboldt, Tennessee, north a Jackson."

The bishop studied the ruddy-faced stranger. "Beat me to Mexico by a few years, I'd say. Looks like you've gone from Tennessee redneck to just plain red all over."

Sterling laughed out loud. "Yessir," he said finally, swaying like a shy schoolboy on his boot edges. "It's all I can do to not catch fire!"

"I'll call you Red then," the bishop said.

"Lots do." Sterling responded, nodding. "I'm in Colonia Estancia about thirty miles yonder north. Holler if you need somethin' and I'll come runnin. It's mighty fine havin' a Mormon ward nearby again. Mighty fine!"

The two men formed an odd bond with few common interests: Tongue-clumsy and bumpkin shy, Red eschewed formality of all kinds and rolled his own cigarettes using a cheap but fragrant pipe tobacco that stunk of rotting flowers and hung in a room long after Red had left it. Smoking was a Mormon taboo; a sin against the body's temple, as was alcohol. Red's take on drinking was on the surreptitious side; he did it when perceiving no one was around to notice. A nip of Tennessee whiskey from a glovebox bottle suited him when called upon, which was often.

Edwin, raised to strict Mormon standards of earthly purity for heavenly reward, wasn't inclined to be judgmental especially from the pulpit. Preaching intolerance was a purview better left to Baptists, he reckoned, and he willingly gave Red and the other Mormon expatriates the kind of breathing room Mexico accustomed them to.

When they argued at all, the topic was usually polygamy, which Edwin viewed as a relic of "old" Mormonism, practiced by a fringe faction.

Red shrugged at that. He couldn't understand why Mormon men wouldn't want to share their bed with many women.

"If you can corral 'em, you get to ride 'em," he told the bishop.

"Red, you're a heathen," the bishop chastised with a shake of his head. "Next Sunday, bring along those wives."

Dutifully Red did. Driving one-handed, his free left arm drooped along the door edge, he eased his red convertible Ford Fairlane into the dusty parking lot and then ran his hand along the fins spiking off the back as he sauntered to the passenger door. Two women both younger by a decade than Red and cedar-post skinny fussed over their wind-blown hair and waited in simple one-piece dresses buttoned to the neck. They looked modest as pageant day schoolmarms; to their scuffed black shoes, laced to the ankles, that crimped their toes and made them squirm during services in their cafeteria seats.

"This here's Delia, my first wife. Goes by Del," Red drawled to the bishop afterward. "And thisn's Samantha. Sam for short."

Edwin beamed as he shook their hands. "Del and Sam, huh? How do you like those nicknames, ladies?" he asked.

Samantha smiled back. "Sam's alright, I guess. Was brung up with four brothers."

"Del's all I ever know'd, sir," said Delia.

As he looked them over, Edwin thought they acted like sisters, so similar were their mannerisms.

Red sensed as much and spoke up. "These gals grew up not more'n twenty miles from each other. Raised up respectful like. Kinda quiet, too, unless I rile 'em."

"Well, let's not do that, shall we?" Edwin laughed. "A pleasure, ladies. Hope to see more of you."

In those early days Edwin oversaw renovation to the old school, which was shuttered following the advance of warehouses and industrial sprawl that pushed the older neighborhood families out. The tar and gravel roof got a repatch, windows caulk and paint, walls a coat of whitewash. The bishop hired work crews to renovate and resupply the cafeteria and ward members did much of the rest, volunteering their time and watching carefully for the scorpions living in the cinderblock walls that creeped out with the morning dew until eventually the sulfur treatments petrified them in their dens.

Across the parking lot from the school, an olio of trade stalls drew Mexican workers every sunup except Sunday, when it was eerily quiet and Edwin, who slept on a cot in his office, indulged himself with an extra cup of coffee.

Shunned as an addiction, coffee was the one vice Edwin sinned over without apology; there were bigger sins to pray over than caffeine.

The coffee stirred Edwin to action and on that day, he pressed his slacks, buffed a shine to his loafers and lingered at the mirror, running fingers through wavy mahogany hair parted down the middle to cover a bald spot on his crown. The thinning hair made him frown and betrayed a younger man's energy of purpose. At services, counting heads, he noted two new families in attendance with children squirming in their folded chairs. He made a mental note to hurry his plans for kindergarten classes.

Each week young Mormons from the States and Central America were dispatched as bilingual missionaries to Edwin's care. Twenty in all, they were given refuge in the homes of other Mormons or they bunked in the empty classrooms. By June, when the lettering for the Church of Jesus Christ of Latter-Day Saints was anchored in Spanish on the school's front wall and the spring rains had yielded to a cloudless blue sky, a knock at Edwin's office door on a late afternoon caught him daydreaming at his desk.

"Come," the bishop said, burying his head back in the Book of Mormon.

The door creaked open and a young woman cradling a baby peered in. Furtively she stepped inside and seeing the bishop quickly knelt with head bowed, paying homage as she would for a priest.

"Please," he said in Spanish. "Stand up. How may I help you?"

Thin and gaunt, she was garbed in a faded striped blouse and long skirt. Bony fingers clutched at the baby wrapped in newspapers wet with urine. Edwin guessed the mother's age at thirty-five; the baby was a newborn. Through her blouse he could see the mother's nipples jutting outward from recent suckling.

"Father," she mouthed, still kneeling with eyes fixed on the floor. "I have two more at home. I must work. There is no money." The bishop stared, a bewildered look on his face. He opened his mouth as if to speak but instead, like a camera on a tripod snap-snapping in auto mode, he simply recorded it all.

When she summoned the courage to meet his gaze, tears trailed down her cheeks and splashed on the floor. She held the baby out to him then, arms raised skyward as in some ancient ritual of sacrifice.

"No!" Edwin stammered, realizing what was happening. But he rose too quickly and clumsily tipped his chair over. Startled, the mother pulled the baby close and rising, made a move to leave.

"Wait. I . . . I want to help," he said. He leaned down and righted the chair while his mind whirled as if it, too, had been tipped out of kilter. What do I say? Should I go to her?

She looked at him hollowly. In faded denim and khakis, he hardly looked priestly to her and, for the briefest moment, she pondered whether she'd entered the wrong room. She scanned it for clues; a coat hanger with no priestly robes upon it, a cot (of all things in a holy man's room!) along a far wall near a table with framed photos of a woman smiling back at her. Her gaze returned to Edwin's desk cluttered with papers and books and then back to the bishop, who seemed frozen on his feet. With her watery eyes, she saw him as through a veil.

"Where is your husband? Your family?" the bishop

finally asked.

"I have heard my husband sleeps with whores!" she said, wiping her eyes with a shirt sleeve. "His partner tells me this. They lay bricks. They crossed to Texas for work. His partner came back a month ago but my husband, he no here. He sends no money. He has forgotten us!"

Edwin fished for his wallet. "Our church is small, but I can give you $20 for food," he said. "How about a blanket for the baby?"

The baby stirred and like a primal cue, something was triggered in the young mother. She shifted her gaze, rescanning the tiny office until her eyes settled on a photo of Gabby smiling from beneath a wide-brimmed gardener's bonnet outside their Utah home. The young mother moved toward it and with her free hand brushed along Gabby's face through the glass.

"I go now," she said then and walked briskly out, closing the door behind her. Surprised by her hasty exit, Edwin hesitated for the briefest moment. When he reached the hall to follow, she was gone.

Then he heard it; at the end of the corridor, first a whimper, agitated grunts and then the clear sharp wail of a baby.

CHAPTER 4

1974 - THE FIXER

Lounging on the back porch stoop, Red took a pull on his cigarette and watched the chickens peck the ground. He counted thirteen, one less than the day before; a matter of little mystery since it was Sam's night to cook and fried chicken was her specialty. The victim crackled in the hot oil inside and the aroma escaped beyond the house to the walled-in yard. Red could smell only a hint of it; years of smoking had dulled his senses.

But not his thinking. Red was a fixer, a wrench in life's trade. As a boy in Humboldt, he fixed lawn mowers and graduated to souping up cars; in the service in California he fixed it so GIs could buy on credit at the PX where he worked (for a fee that he pocketed). As a college student on the GI Bill, he fixed cheat sheets for friends that helped them pass and made them beholden. He offered fixes in the business world that colleagues debated as resourceful or just plain crooked. Whenever accused of the latter, Red simply found another town to do business in.

His fix for marriage was Mormonism, because life was

unbearable in the company of just one woman. Past relationships taught Red that the more time a man spends with a woman, the more things she could think for him to do. Two wives instead of one wasn't twice the trouble, it was half as much in Red's mind since he gave each half as much attention. Having a third wife would be even better, he figured, and he was always on the lookout for a new one. With three he would hardly have time to talk with them at all.

Red rose from the porch stoop just as the phone rang in the kitchen. "It's Bishop Youngblood," Sam said distractedly. The flame on the chicken was hotter than she intended and grease was spattering the stovetop.

On the other end, Edwin breathed into the phone, winded. "How are your wives with babies?"

"Huh?" Red queried. "We got no kids. You know that!"

"Well, it just so happens I do," the bishop said. He held the phone away from his ear and Red could make out high-pitched crying in the adjacent classroom as a cafeteria worker tended the child. "A week old, I think. Mother left her in the hall."

"My, my," said Red.

"Yeah. I was wondering if your wives could care for her a few days 'til I can figure something out."

Red was silent. "Sure thing," he said finally. "Be right over."

In the forty-five minutes it took Red and his wives to wheel the older model Fairlane into the church parking lot, Edwin had sent a staff member to the mercado for baby bottles, formula, and diapers. The baby was asleep when Sam and Del bounded down the hall and into Edwin's office.

"Shh," Edwin admonished, holding his finger to his lips. Laid out on a blanket on the floor beside the bishop's desk, the baby had been swaddled tightly in a bed sheet. Delia scooped her up in seconds and headed unceremoniously toward the car, with Sam close behind.

Edwin watched in amazement.

"Truth is," Red told the bishop, "they've been wanting to get in a family way and I've been puttin' it off. So they jumped all over this deal."

"I see," said Edwin. "Tell them not to grow too attached. I haven't called the police yet, but I fully intend to."

"Might wanna rethink that, Bishop," Red responded. "Orphanages in Mexico are no bueno. Gotta trust me on this."

"But the police can track down his mother and make her take her baby back," Edwin said, exasperated.

"You're a good man, Bishop. Can see that a mile away," said Red. "But people don't get found in Mexico unless they wanna be."

Edwin was silent. Reflecting back on the brief encounter, it was clear the baby's mother was in a desperate state when she came to him; likely drawn by some hope the church would take in her child. But why?

"Any idea how the Catholic church deals with these situations?" Edwin asked.

"They call the police," Red said. "Wash their hands of it."

"So why might she think it would be any different at our church?"

"Don't rightly know, Bishop. Your church is fillin' up. Hard to say what the street talk is."

The bishop considered Red's notion of things and decided to give the matter more thought. He shook Red's hand and sent him after his wives.

That evening, Edwin fixed a sandwich in the cafeteria and strode back to his office, where he slouched in his chair in his evening attire, faded shorts and a T-shirt. He propped his feet atop the desk and with the sandwich in his lap on a napkin, he took slow bites and mulled things. Though his station in life meant he was sometimes called upon to find some heavenly logic in the randomness of daily life, Edwin rarely found the words without leaning on the wisdom of others. His main confidant was Gabby who, though not as worldly as Edwin, was a problem solver; good at finding the nub in knotty matters. Edwin had discovered her talents at Brigham Young when she taught him to find order in the chaos of chemistry. They had been thrown together as lab mates when Edwin was confounded by the Periodic Table of Elements, which everyone had to memorize.

"Break it up into pieces. Start with metals, like iron, with a symbol of Fe," she had told him. "Ferocious, right? Silver is Ag as in . . . well, think of a silver farm, having to do with agriculture. It's a rote memory exercise. Turn it into a game."

Reaching Gabby that evening, Edwin described his encounter with the mother. When he finished, she was silent.

"Well?" said Edwin.

"That's the saddest story ever," she said finally, blowing her nose into a tissue and dabbing moistened eyes. "She had nowhere to turn. Nowhere at all."

Edwin nodded. "The husband's deserted them, I guess,

the bastard!"

"Is that appropriate talk for a bishop?" Gabby scolded. "Life's unfair is all. No mother should have to go through that! Deserting one child so she can feed the rest? God forgive her!"

"God placed this child in my hands," Edwin said. "I hope the mother can forgive herself."

Gabby, seated in a wing-backed chair in the couple's Utah den, listened to the chatter of two squirrels playing tag in the ash and oak trees of the gated backyard. Then a thought hatched and she rose to her feet.

"What you just said, Edwin, about having that baby's fate in your hands . . . think about it. We can't have children. Maybe God wants us to have this one! Maybe this is a new calling! Could it be? Could it?"

From its cradle Edwin's phone slipped from between his collarbone and chin and landed in his lap. He picked it back up and gazed into the receiver. "You mean, just keep her?" he asked.

"I sure do," she said. "Why not?"

"There are a hundred reasons why not," he said, incredulous. "She belongs to the mother. If not her, then there's bound to be a grandmother or uncle who'll want her. Besides that, how could we raise her while I'm here and you're there running our business?"

Gabby sighed into the phone. "The great Bishop Youngblood! You talk a blue streak, but you don't always listen. Maybe God's talking to you, Edwin."

"God's busier than we are, you know?" he said. "This isn't divine intervention, hon. It's a sad reality of everyday life in Mexico. We can't adopt every child who needs us anymore than we can save every soul.

"I will say this," Edwin added. "When I heard that baby crying in the hall this afternoon, I was scared. I mean like what do I do now? I thought 'I could sure use Gabby here'."

"You better be glad I wasn't there," she said. "Red's wives would have had a tough time prying that baby from my arms."

"I think I should see one of these Mexican orphanages for myself," the bishop said after a moment of silence between them. "They can't be as bad as people say."

- - -

Durango's only orphanage, a fenced-in compound of six faded white concrete buildings on the eastern edge of town, was unadvertised and unadorned. It drooped like a white-haired sentry on a porch swing expecting visitors who hadn't come. Edwin imposed on Elder John Speck to drive and accompany him on a tour offered only to local clergy.

It was mid-morning. Feeding time was delayed in the crib ward because two workers called in sick. Before Edwin and John stepped inside, they could hear the babies screaming. They eyed one another, girded themselves and entered.

Their noses flared with the stink of soiled diapers and Lysol in the low-ceilinged crib room, where four large room fans churned the stale air, which had nowhere to go since the windows were sealed. Two middle-aged women with cotton stuffed in their ears moved about the four rows of cribs with purpose, selectively feeding and burping based on scream volume. A third worker was heating water on a hot plate and mixing formula. The bishop and his elder squinted at the auditory invasion.

"We have to help," John, a short and portly father of

four, said loudly to Edwin. He turned quickly, grabbed formula, and began feeding a baby swaddled in a blue and red striped hospital blanket. It sucked hungrily. Edwin lifted an infant and pressed it to his chest. As he rocked it gently, the baby settled down. He looked upon its face and began a soothing lullaby using whispered words. The baby's eyes searched his. The bishop laid it down, wiped a moistened eye with his hand and instantly felt his eye burning. He looked down and realized both hands were wet with urine and feces.

In the next building, larger and taller than the crib room, all the children had shaved heads because of a lice infestation. A plaque above the dormitory entrance read: **Train up a child in the way he should go: and when he is old, he will not depart from it. Proverbs 22:6.** These were the children the orphanage considered most adoptable and there were dozens in the main room, ranging in age from three to eight. The girls, in pullover cotton dresses and the boys, in T-shirts and denim shorts, ran barefoot to the men, grabbing at their arms and legs.

"I go home with you?" asked one girl of Edwin in English. "I am five." Her tiny fingers were swallowed by his big right hand, so she wrapped her hand around his index finger and squeezed.

"No, me," said another in Spanish, pulling on the bishop's other arm. "I'm pretty!"

Two boys clung to John's pants legs and sat on his shoes.

"Give us a ride," one said. "We are brothers." When he took some steps forward, they squealed with excitement.

There seemed so many that Edwin was riveted. The children, oblivious to their ragged appearance, tugged his shirt and sleeves with dirty hands vying for attention. With their shaved heads, they looked like concentration camp children the bishop had seen in World War II newsreels. But these children were smiling, posing for Edwin and John, as they had done dozens of times when potential adoptive parents called; as their orphanage administrators had taught them. Posing was their ticket out; there was no other.

On a folding table in a corner, workers were preparing a lunch of corn tortillas and bowls of beans. Plastic cups contained red Kool Aid. An aide announced, "Lunch. Line up" and whoosh, the children abandoned the men and took their places in the serving line. The room was suddenly quiet; there was no talking in line.

The bishop spied a little girl standing in solitude beside a window spotted on the outside with splash marks from a recent rain. A spider scurrying up the windowsill had caught her eye and she didn't notice as Edwin neared.

"Aren't you hungry," the bishop asked in Spanish.

"Yes," she said. She was tall and skinny with a puggish nose and large round eyes. Edwin squatted beside her and asked about the bandage on her right wrist. The eight-year-old bowed her head in embarrassment. "Spider bite. Did you know spiders are mean?"

"I think a lot of people are afraid of spiders."

"I am now," she said.

"Does it hurt?"

"No." She turned her hand this way and that before returning her gaze to the window. "The keepers said I can go back to work in a few days."

"Keepers?"

She turned back to Edwin and eyed him curiously.

"They keep us here, so yes. Are you here to adopt one of us?"

"No. I'm a minister. I'll be coming back to see you again, though," Edwin said. "May I ask your name?"

"Consuela."

"That name's as pretty as you are," the bishop said, beaming. Consuela shrugged at the compliment. She refocused on the sill.

"What kind of work do you do for the keepers, Consuela?" he asked.

"I clean at shops and restaurants. Sometimes I ask tourists for money on street corners," she said. "The keepers use the money to pay for our food."

"How is the food?"

"It's just food. The same, always."

"How long have you been here, honey?"

"Always."

The most forlorn of the orphanage occupied the last and largest barracks the two men visited that day. They were the unadoptables; too old or damaged to be wanted and too young to go free. The building had thirty twin bunkbeds and a dayroom with twelve wooden school desks. The sixty occupants were schooled in shifts. All worked outside the orphanage by day or night as dishwashers, maids, or errand boys to local tradesmen.

This would be Consuela's next stop as soon as there was room for her. Classes were underway when Edwin and John entered, and it was quiet inside save for the instructor's monotone as she read from a history book to the twenty-eight boys and girls at their desks. In the center row sat a twelve-year-old boy with one arm, next to a heavy-set girl with an unrepaired cleft palate. Another boy with a cane beside his desk wearing lopsided orthopedic shoes hunched beside a girl with a long purplish birthmark on her forehead and another with a thick mole on her right cheek. The remainder had no outward flaws, but Edwin found it odd that none of the children, not one, acknowledged their presence beside them.

The teacher noticed and counseled the children to tell their guests hello. "Hola," they said as one. One of them smiled at Edwin and John. The others regarded them for a moment without emotion. He sensed a hollowness in the children's eyes, similar to the faraway look he saw from Consuela. In the awkward ensuing moments, the bishop nudged his friend and they took their leave.

Edwin didn't speak on the drive back to the ward. He could not think of a single place or thing that had depressed him more. In his office, he searched for words to describe his feelings. He thought he might fashion a sermon on charity, or adoption. For a full hour he stared at a blank piece of paper. What came to him was this:

A life without purpose is a lamp never lit.

He found some parchment paper and wrote it again, in large letters, like some relic of import. He put it in a frame and hung it behind his desk, where it remained for the rest of the mission.

- - -

Edwin nursed a second cup of coffee at his desk the next morning when Red reached him by phone.

"Bishop, I think I've solved your baby problem," he said. "Did I introduce ya' to my attorney friend up here in my colonia? Name's Marmoles."

"No," Edwin spoke into the phone. "Has he been to the ward?"

"Nope. He's a Methodist . . . nice guy though; retired here a few years back. I run legal errands for him now and then," Red said. "He helps folks when they're in a jam."

"Sounds like a good friend to have," the bishop said.

"Sure is. And Marmoles says that by leavin' that baby on your doorstep, the mother gave up her parental rights. Best thing is to sit tight for a spell, a few weeks maybe, see if she comes back," Red said. "If she don't, then he said find that baby a good home."

"Have you been talking to my wife?" Edwin asked. "She thought we should adopt her."

"Funny you say that," Red said. "Marmoles said there's an adoption agency on the border with connections to the U.S. They could find her a family. Probably a Mormon one if we ask. But if you want her instead, just say the word."

"No thanks Red. Gabby and I may go that route at some point but not now," the bishop said. "Tell you what. If it's legit what your friend Marmoles suggests, I'm okay with it. And I'll call around to the bishops in Provo to see if they know any parents looking to adopt."

"Perfect!" Red said. "I'll git to it."

Red cradled the phone and smiled. The fix was in. The Juarez adoption agency Red had in mind had offered $1,500 for the baby. The only glitch was a birth certificate necessary to make the transaction legal. Red was pretty sure he had a fix for that as well.

CHAPTER 5

THE MIDWIFE

It was too hot to leave the top down on his Fairlane so Red took to driving in an undershirt with the windows open. A jug of Coca-Cola and bourbon in the cup holder sloshed beside him. He dipped a hand towel in a flip-top ice chest of cool water on the passenger side floorboard on occasion and draped it from his neck. When his back and legs stuck to the gritty white Naugahyde upholstery, Red cursed the sun and prayed for rain.

For most of two days Red made a slow creep through the western colonias of Durango, questing a fix for Edwin Youngblood's baby problem. He pulled alongside women he saw and asked them straight up what he wanted.

"Pardon, senora. I need a midwife. Know a good one?" His was a choppy Tex-Mex dialect, passable for Spanish but with a strong southern twang. The women had seen and heard many like him closer to the city where expatriates made up a cross section of the bustling markets there, so they felt no threat from him despite his imposing frame. They told him of the midwives they knew of like Colibri, the "hummingbird", a woman in her sixties who sang reassuringly through childbirths. The expectant mothers liked her bedside manner, but her fees were steep and she limited deliveries to neighborhoods within walking distance of her home. There was Sister Hinojosa, once a Catholic nun, who was said to deliver babies for free on occasion but only for the poorest of the poor. Many spoke of Teresa Cortez, a former delivery nurse from Hospital General de Durango in the city's center who had several nicknames, one of them rooted in her habit of wearing hospital scrubs into the barrios. All were faded orange and with her rounded shape, her navel protruded against them, leading one of the men to dub her ombligo naranja, orange navel. Many more called her enfermera de la noche, the night nurse, or la fantasma, the ghost, because she preferred sleeping by day and making prenatal visits only after dark. Locals regarded her as shadowy and aloof, but Teresa was fond of saying that her real patients, the babies, obliged her nocturnal habits by arriving, quite regularly, just in time for breakfast. It was said Cortez had been banned from the downtown hospital in the 1960s because her bedside manner as a nurse's aide was icy and distant. When asked, Teresa did not deny this and told expectant mothers to expect the same from her in their homes; she had long ago wearied of complaining patients, know-it-all doctors and people in general. In the barrios, though, manners and niceties weren't a required stock in trade. Two things were: Guile as a trusty and sure-handed midwife and Teresa's willingness to accept barter for payment, whether food, clothing, or skilled labor; the latter of which she depended on to turn a walled-in skeleton of a home on inherited property outside Durango into a palatial retreat she fancied moving into someday.

Red found her one evening wheeling an older model Ford Pinto with faded paint through Colonia Francisco with a dirt trail kicking up behind her. She stopped beside a rough-hewn house of adobe without a stick of green around it and disappeared inside. When she came out, Red was nearby, leaning on his car.

"They say you're a ghost," Red said in English. "But I found ya."

"Don't want to be found," she shot back. "Leave me be."

She regarded Red suspiciously. Her left hand slipped inside the bag draped from her shoulder and fumbled for the small knife she kept there.

"Not here to make trouble, Senora Cortez. I heard you're a good midwife. Think I might be needin' one." Red grinned and showed off his crooked front teeth.

"You either need a midwife or you don't," Teresa corrected. "There's no might be."

Red took a step toward her, reconsidered, then clumsily rested his stubby thumbs in his jean pockets. "It's true that licensed midwives can sign birth certificates and get 'em recorded with the courts, ain't it?"

"It's true enough," she said, reaching for her car door.

"Then I need one," Red said. "Please hear me out, ma'am. Name's Sterling Pierce and I'm part of a church trying to grow some roots here in Durango. Maybe you've heard of the Mormon Church out of Utah. Takin' the world by storm, it is, and the local bishop, a fella named Youngblood, he's a man of vision.

"I'm here 'cause a woman left a baby at his church doorstep. Damn fine one, too. Here, have a look," he said, stepping slightly forward to hand her a photograph.

Teresa opened her car door and eyed the photo in the dim cabin light. She chuckled at the bed sheet swaddling and wordlessly handed it back.

"A Juarez adoption agency's found a home for her in the States," he continued. "Offerin' a thousand bucks American for the baby but they need a birth certificate to make it all legal-like. And nobody knows who the mother is."

"You want me to make one up then?" she asked. "That why you're here?"

Red pulled off his sweat-stained Stetson, reached above his ear for the cigarette he'd rolled and lit it. "I'm askin' ya to give this baby a chance, that's all. The bishop named her Hope . . . you know, Esperanza," Red continued. "Lord knows she could use some."

"Who couldn't?" she shot back. "So what?"

"What ya get for a delivery hereabouts?" Red queried. "A hunnert, two maybe? Well, thisn's already born. I'll give you four hunnert just for sayin' so. And you'll save her as sure as if you'd pulled her breach from a dyin' mother's belly."

Teresa remained silent and closely eyed Red while he wiped his brow with the wet towel on his neck. A drop of water fell onto the tip of the cigarette dangling from the side of his mouth, putting it out. He let it fall from his lips to the ground.

"Here's how it is, mister" she said finally. "I make decent money doing what I do. It's not always enough but as you can see I don't miss many meals. Anything extra comes along, I'm grateful. But you're askin' me to risk my license for you and this baby. Something goes wrong, I lose my livelihood. That's a bad bargain. Now it's time I was on my way." She stepped into the car and slipped her key in the ignition.

Red stepped to her open window. "I get it. You need to think on it. I'll give you five hunnerd instead of four. How 'bout that?" He reached in his pocket and handed Teresa a piece of paper with his phone number on it. "We do this deal," he said, "and they'll be more. Enough to finish that house folks say you're buildin'. Think on it. When you call, ask for Red."

On the way home, Teresa Cortez turned up the radio and mouthed the words to a Mexican song, "No Tengo Dinero". As she neared her two-room apartment on the edge of downtown, she changed course suddenly and drove east until the city lights faded behind her. The highway climbed the foothills of the Sierra Madre like a sidewinder. In time, she turned northward along a tiny dirt road that led to a cattle guard and just past it, adobe bricks stacked into walls overlooking the city. She left the car running so the lights could guide her steps and carried a flashlight. A rattler caught in the open coiled and whipped its tail in warning as the headlight washed over it. The nurse saw it and trudged annoyedly back to the car, retrieving a .38 pistol from her glovebox. She returned and dispatched the snake with the pop! pop! of gunfire. She watched it writhe and contort then stepped to the low-walled courtyard where she envisioned a fountain someday cascading beside lush plants and native flowers by walkways of terrazzo tile. The bricks to the home itself climbed only a few feet in places, interspersed with framing wood rising skeleton-like above the clay. The bricks outlined where the floor to ceiling windows would someday face the courtyard. Stakes in the ground marked bedrooms, a roomy kitchen and den. It was to be a large house in the style of adobe ranches she'd seen in magazines.

She faced the city glowing like flickering neon far below. She loved this perch of land with its rock outcroppings and knotted oaks where the desert began its retreat from the higher mesas that formed the foothills. She loved looking down on Durango, from her perch and metaphorically, too. She had long ago tired of the city; its richness eluded her all her life. The cathedrals of the inner city, the bustling streets and shops, were like a postcard from somewhere else. The Durango Teresa knew was hard and gritty; it was open toilets and fire pits and undrinkable water, summers without air conditioning, winters without firewood; bloody knuckles and unwashed hands and aprons cut into diapers.

"No soul," she muttered. "You work and you die. That's all. If it weren't for this patch of ground, I don't think I could stand another day."

She thought of Red's offer. She sloshed it around like spit and then stammered, "Doin' it!"

Her voice bounced off the hillside and returned to her. A smile curled around her fat cheeks. She turned back to the shell of a home and she saw instead a magnificent walled fortress covered with fine adobe plaster with a tile roof laid upon huge hand carved cedar posts and stone floors bathed in fine imported rugs. There were servants moving about as she sat at the head of a long dining room table and feasted on what they brought her. She could almost taste it.

"Doin' it," she whispered and ambled to her dust-caked car.

An urgent phone call awaited Teresa at home. A mother of twins was in hard labor. On a mat on the floor of a hut built mostly of sheet metal, Cortez brought life to one and lost the second whose umbilical cord was wrapped around his neck. Cortez rested both babies on their mother's breasts and whispered, "Rosalita, this is your brother Manuel. He's watching you from Heaven. And he always will." Unceremoniously she took Manuel from the crying mother and cocooned him in a baby blanket. There were forms to fill out on both the birth and death. The father, a day laborer, stared at the palms of his hands in a corner of the lamp-lit room. He had wondered aloud for weeks how the couple could afford to feed two children. But as he watched the light cast flickering shadows over the tools of his trade, he felt only the anguish of losing a son.

The labor and deliveries lasted eight hours. Cortez took Manuel to the city morgue and arrived at her apartment at 5:35 a.m. She slipped off her shoes at the door and padded past her nineteen-year-old daughter, Juanita, lying uncovered in a long T-shirt on a sofa sleeper in the living room. Long brown hair covered much of her face. The midwife brushed her teeth in her bathroom and collapsed into bed fully clothed.

CHAPTER 6

2002 – DAY ONE

A sleepy Mexican wind drifting from the Pacific onto the half-covered veranda swayed the hammock gently where Ruben Youngblood dozed, his body slunk in the webbing, arms across his chest, lazily overlapping at the wrists as in a death pose.

From her perch atop the terraza railing, wife Rebecca listened to the sputtering engines of the fishing boats slipping unseen from the ocean into the calm bay waters below. As they neared the tiny harbor of Zihuatanejo, where a string of lightbulbs illuminated a solitary dock, she could make out the dull white hulls of them slicing through the black water and, farther in, she saw the pescaderos waiting to bargain over catches of roosterfish, grouper and snapper to be hauled in wheelbarrows to the hotels of nearby Ixtapa and the village restaurants that catered to the tourists.

From her vantage point, Rebecca could not see the beach directly below the Soto Vento, their hotel. Their room was four floors up, so she saw instead the open-air restaurant just below her pointing toes, where some guests still supped. The lobby stood at the same level as the mountain road that meandered above the bay and into the village itself a quarter mile to the north. Straining toward the darkness, Rebecca traced the faint outline of the Playa la Ropa on the bay's southern edge, still visible despite a cloud-masked moon and so named, according to legend, for the day centuries before when a shipwreck's contents of linens washed ashore there. Closer in, a small herd of cattle lay on the cool sea-washed sand. Across the bay and up the mountainside, the warm lights of the village flickered and danced; some musty streetlights, others latched to walls or strung haphazardly from solitary trees behind houses of adobe or concrete block. From time to time, Rebecca could hear a muffler-less taxi pass along the road and drown out the cadence of the boats. But for that, the evening was calm and sweet with the scent of idleness.

She threw a glance over her shoulder at Ruben, his face half-covered by a Panama hat, his dark and bone-thin body in repose. It seemed to Rebecca that Mexico wore well on him. On their second day below the border, he purchased the hat, peasant sandals and two summer weight shirts that hung loosely over his shoulders; the one he had on was badly wrinkled, but it made him seem all the more native in it. In the village today, she had noticed, he sauntered about with lazy legs as if feeling the ground beneath his feet and testing its texture, loving the pace of the sleepy town, oblivious to a destination. And though Ruben was of Mexican descent, these habits were new.

Somewhat unsettled by Mexico, Rebecca was a cautious tourist. What she knew of the country had come from books. She'd read of the contrasts along the U.S.-Mexico border; of sewerless slums on the Mexican side reeking from packing houses that shipped their beef to travertine-tiled American kitchens across the Rio Grande; of corruption as foul as any odor permeating the Mexican political system; of provinces run by drug lords in a country flush with oil; of dreamy landscapes teeming with pockets of poverty like ant hills in a fragrant meadow.

The only child of an American-born Mexican couple, Rebecca's land was America. She grew up speaking English at home, never Spanish. It was important to her parents, Joe and Angeline Vega, that she be as American as anyone in their neighborhood on the outskirts of Provo, Utah. She wore blue taffeta to the fourth-grade pageant when she played Cinderella; hosted her entire seventh-grade class at the local water park for her birthday and played *Kirby's Dream Land* on Game Boy with them in her rec room in ninth grade while Angeline captured it all on video and Joe burned CDs in time to include them in their goody bags.

In college, when peers spoke of inheriting a world on the brink of collapse, she was the voice of hope.

"Everyone's starving in the world," a political science major at Brigham Young University remarked over pizza in the quad. "They're eating rats in Naples."

"Which is why," Rebecca said dismissively, "the pope lives in Rome."

She could not help herself; turning negatives to positives was a Vega specialty. Naples and Rome were mere dots on a map in a world full of promise; where good intentions trump bad ones; where, as it was for Roman gladiators, a mere thumbs up could snatch victory from defeat.

Sudden laughter from the restaurant wafted into Ruben's ears. Opening one eye, he gazed at the inside of his hat. Reluctantly, he raised the brim and smiled at his good fortune—it was Rebecca's rear end he saw, taut against her white shorts as she leaned from the railing to eavesdrop on the restaurant below.

"My, my," said a voice from the hammock.

Rebecca blushed. The shorts she'd donned after dinner were skimpier than a Mormon wife typically wore. "Enjoying the view, sailor?"

"Indeed. Those shorts new?" he queried.

"Thought they'd be okay to wear around the house. Don't know how they got in my suitcase." She felt his eyes upon her so she took a seat in the wicker chair near him and fidgeted with the dahlia bloom she'd plucked from the nightstand vase and slipped into her hair. Ruben, she noticed, was grinning under the hat, though his eyes remained in shadow.

"You coming out of there any time soon?" she asked.

"Naw. I'm one with the hammock." He feigned a yawn.

"We still have to pack you know," she reminded. "Tomorrow's the big day."

The nightstand telephone rang, bleating through the wood framed mesh screen that separated the room from the veranda, it seemed insistent against the evening's calm and Rebecca hurried to answer it. "Hello? Hi, Edwin, how are you? We're fine. It's lovely here."

On the other end, Edwin Youngblood was animated. They hadn't spoken since he saw them off at the Provo airport.

"I'm so glad," he said. "Weather's good? Your day was

good?"

"Hot for sure but the ocean breeze helps a lot," said Rebecca. "Great day for us. So how's my munchkin? She still awake?"

"Of course, of course," Edwin said. He cupped the phone and called to his wife Gabby to pick up. In a moment, Rebecca could hear Megan breathing into the phone.

"Is that you, sweetheart?"

"Hi Mommy. Mamaw and me were reading Night Night Moon," Megan cooed. "And I rode a bike today all by myself! Pawpa and Mamaw got it for me."

"Really," said her mother. "Training wheels come with it?"

"Uh huh. It's got a bell too and sparkly things on the grips. And it's not even my birthday!"

"Our baby got a bicycle today," Rebecca announced to Ruben as he strode up beside her.

"Baby? She's almost four," Ruben corrected.

"She'll sleep good tonight," Edwin chimed in. "We all will."

Rebecca laughed. "Thanks for doing this, Edwin. It's been a wonderful break. Now munchkin, it's time you and Mamaw finished that book. And then it's time for bed. I'll see you tomorrow. Love you bunches."

"Bye, bye" Megan said quickly, itching to get back to Goodnight Moon, her favorite.

Rebecca handed the phone to Ruben. "So was there a sale on bicycles at Toys "R" Us?" he said to his father. "Or did you just need her out of the house?"

Edwin chuckled. "She's been a joy. Are you geared up for tomorrow?"

"Mixed feelings. This place, Zihuatanejo, is amazing. I could stay for months. But yeah, Durango calls."

"I do hope you find her," Edwin said, turning serious. "It's likely you won't, I think, but there's a chance. If you do . . . we've talked about this already, I know, but . . ." He paused. "I just worry how she'll react. I knew very little about Rosa Segovia. I knew next to nothing about most of them."

"Dad, I get it. We've hashed and rehashed this," Ruben said. "I'm twenty-five now and I've been talking about this since college. You've discouraged it, all along."

"I wouldn't say that," Edwin said defensively. "Maybe I have, I don't know. There's plenty of work waiting for you at the office. Maybe you should be hurrying back to that."

"And I will, soon enough," Ruben said impatiently, "But for now, I'm going to find my birth mother and tell her how much I hate my boss."

"Not funny," Edwin said. "Just hurry back, okay?"

Ruben cradled the phone and eyed Rebecca amorously. "I need a drink. How 'bout you."

"You don't drink."

"A Coke then. With lime," Ruben suggested. "Speaking of limes, wasn't that amazing what the cab driver did today?"

Rebecca smiled. "Scary at first," she recalled. "I mean, you mention in the cab we forgot to buy limes and before we knew it, we're off the main road and this guy's taking us to the sticks. And some of those houses were literally made of sticks."

"Yeah, but we pull up in front of his house," said Ruben, "and he grabs us five limes from his tree in the back yard. Now that was cool!"

"And he wouldn't take a dime," Rebecca marveled.

Ruben rummaged in his cargo shorts. "Here we go. Two left." He rolled the limes in his hand.

"Is there anything you don't have stashed in those shorts?" she asked, running her fingers through her shoulder length hair.

"Still got a few things you might be interested in," he baited. "Two balls and a nine iron. Care to play a round?"

Rebecca blushed again. "More like a putter. I'll get the Cokes." She grabbed the ice bucket. "Start packing."

Picking her way along the stairs, she threw a smile at a couple working their way up from the beach. "My husband," she told them, "is crazy!" They stared wordlessly and Rebecca wondered if they spoke English. "Muy bonkers," she offered instead.

When she returned Ruben was shirtless and lounging on the bed, watching the blades of the ceiling fan paint huge shadows on the whitewashed walls of the simple room with two small nightstands and a worn dresser against a wall where suitcase racks sagged under the weight of their belongings. Two padded chairs and an end table with a Bible and Book of Mormon on top hugged the far wall. There was no TV; no phone; no air conditioning. The ocean breezes cooled the room through the mesh screen.

Rebecca brought the Cokes and joined Ruben on the bed. He got up to cut the limes then squeezed some into each glass. "Kinda glad we can't drink the water here," he said, plopping back down. "What's better than a lime Coke?"

They sipped and were silent, allowing the ceiling fan's

hypnotic whir, cooling the evening air like an angel's breath, to recast the spell of Zihuatanejo. Rebecca closed her eyes and shifted her head until it rested on her husband's shoulder.

"This is nice," she purred and she slipped her right arm around his lower back.

"Wanna fool around?" he asked quickly, sensing opportunity.

"Let's just hold each other a while."

"Okay." Sliding his shoulder from beneath her, he put down his Coke and nestled his head against her breasts then ran fingers along her shorts hem. He grazed the birthmark on her left hip. Just a hint of it showed. He unzipped her shorts part way and exposed it.

"Your birthmark looks exactly like a quarter moon," he said.

"It's a crescent moon," she corrected.

"Has Megan ever noticed? You know how much she loves Goodnight Moon."

"I don't think so," she said. "It never occurred to me."

He leaned in and kissed her birthmark, tasting it with his tongue.

"No craters on this moon," he advised.

"You're being naughty," she cautioned. "Crawl back up here and use that tongue to kiss me."

Still at his desk, Edwin stared at the phone and pouted. The sense of dread that had haunted him for weeks was now popping his ears. He pinched his nose, held his breath and puffed his cheeks to relieve the pressure but it was no use. His mind was clogged with worry.

Slouching in his high-backed leather chair, he noticed the belt of his robe was pressing on his belly. He loosened the cinch, sat up and plopped his arms exaggeratedly onto the armrests.

Ruben was the son of a mother he did not know. He was bestowed on Edwin and Gabby by Teresa Cortez, a midwife he knew well but hardly trusted. The adoption that came of it was legalized in El Paso, though Ruben was born in Durango. It had held up for twenty-five years, but Edwin knew better than anyone just how fragile such arrangements could be.

He reached into his desk drawer and retrieved a folder bulging with loose papers, grabbing the one on top, a letter, that began "Dear Bishop Youngblood, Our Gilberto just blessed us with our first grandchild, Julio. He's fat-cheeked and plumb all over! What a healthy joy of a boy (guess I'm a poet, huh?).

"Since I wrote last, our son graduated with honors from Yale with a degree in mechanical engineering. He has a good job and stands six feet five inches tall but is gentle as a lamb and happy as a clam! (there I go again!). He and Cynthia are in Boston now, loving the turning of the leaves.

"Just can't thank you enough, Edwin, for the blessing of this fine man. Hope all is well with you and Gabby and Ruben. Love, Vanessa Cartwright. Phoenix"

Another letter spoke of "the miracle" of a daughter and how she'd become a doctor in Salt Lake City, Utah. "You brought the miracle to us, Bishop Youngblood. You're a saint. Love, Anne Patterson."

He closed the folder and placed it back in the drawer.

So many adoptions. So many Rubens and Marias and Javiers and Catalinas with my fingerprints on them who now, as adults, may be burning to know their birth mothers.

What would come of it, he wondered.

Edwin kicked at the desk backing with his house shoes, then padded sullenly upstairs.

CHAPTER 7

2002 – DAY TWO

The plane trip to Mexico City made Rebecca queasy. The airport out of Ixtapa was near the mountains so the pilots had to ascend quickly, pressing the passengers against their seat backs. The cabin air flow was weak and, dressed in slacks and blouse with a thin half sweater, Rebecca felt sweat beading along her back.

"What will we do when we land in Durango?" she asked over the droning engines.

"Durango's an industrial city; really spread out," he said. "The address I have for my mother doesn't show up on any maps I could find on the internet. Might take a day or two to find it."

Rebecca winced. Beyond the majestic mountains below them was a vast interior to Mexico that in summer kiln-baked much of the land. The city of Durango, at a slightly higher elevation on the edge of the Sierra Madre, fared better than other interior spots, with summer temperatures typically no worse than 95 degrees. But rugged wastelands lay on all sides of the city, in places where movie stars made spaghetti westerns among the scrub, mesquite, bluffs and gorges carved from rock and hardpan soil.

When Ruben first broached the trip to Mexico, the movie lore of Durango Rebecca discovered online prompted her to stream *The Good, the Bad and the Ugly* onto her computer. The state of Durango, where most of the movie was filmed, looked to Rebecca as inhospitable in the western as fictional depictions of Mars, with dust-devil tornadoes raging over a barren red landscape.

She rested her eyes and tried to erase the image from her mind. She turned to Ruben, who looked to be napping, and placed her hand over his, squeezing it lightly. He acknowledged her with a smile but kept his eyes shut. He was trying to make sense of the dream the night before. He'd found himself alone in a barrio that ran forever toward the horizon until, from the edge of his dreamworld dozens of Mexican peasant women appeared carrying babies they begged him to take. They came and came, nudging their children toward him. From nowhere a car rolled up and a woman with black pools for eyes began grabbing the offered babies and tossing them screaming into the backseat while the mothers ran behind, scooping up the wads of pesos the woman was tossing out the car window. The sound of crying stayed with him even after the dream had jolted him awake. Craning his neck above his pillow he had realized the wakeful crying was coming from a baby in an adjacent room of the hotel. The child's mother was singing to it in Spanish.

Rebecca reopened her eyes, unable to sleep on the plane. She turned back to the window and squinted into it. In front and below the plane was an orange haze, nudging closer. As the plane started its descent, the haze was upon them, now brownish and soup-like. "Are those rain clouds?" Rebecca asked Ruben. "They look so dirty."

"Smog," he said. "The summer heat traps it over the city. It's some of the worst in the world."

"It's like flying into a smokestack," she said, averting her gaze.

On the ground in Mexico City, Rebecca regarded the polluted skies out the terminal window and felt a longing for home. An hour later they were whisked in an Aero Mexico jet to Durango that arrived by three. Exiting the small terminal to find their rental car, they were unprepared for the heat, which whooshed across their faces as the exit door slid open. "Whoa," said Ruben, feeling it flare his nostrils and lungs. Hotter still was the car, an older model blue Chevy, baking in a shadeless parking lot.

"Okay, this sucks," he said, settling into the car. The ocean breezes they'd enjoyed in Zihuatanejo were a distant memory. He tinkered with the car's air conditioner which produced a constant stream of warm air.

Ruben had an address for a map store in the city and made for it, windows down. A mapmaker he encountered claimed to know the city's barrios well. Though there was more than one Calle Rubio in Durango, the store owner suggested one in Colonia Francisco, the poorest barrio. That one, he told Ruben, had a long history of neglect.

"If your mother was there when you were born," the owner told him, "she is probably there now, if she is not dead."

CHAPTER 8

1974

July arrived in a pantyhose disguise; one pair, two intruders, 2 a.m.

Robbers did a walkabout of the church with flashlights after discovering the front door unlocked and, misguided into thinking Mormons prayed to a God different than theirs, feared for nothing. The fear was all Edwin Youngblood's, who awoke to the flashlights' glare. The men stood over his cot, shouting orders and frightening the bishop so much he would discover afterward that he had wet himself. The men took his wallet, his computer and some food stock from the kitchen and were gone. Edwin told his elders there were guns involved but in truth he couldn't recall seeing one.

It was the time of year when summer settled over Durango like a long siesta, turning the activities of day and night upside down. People sleep-walked by day but by nightfall were restless pinatas waiting for the moon glow to animate or burst them open. Crimes big and small became night crimes. The sun by day sapped all but the saplings, the youngest of the young, and those working outside turned sloth-like.

It was all Edwin could do to coax his missionaries back to the streets that first summer. They sweated in their cots and woke to a melon-ripe sun. The U.S.-born volunteers were the worst: They begged Edwin to let them sleep the afternoon heat away as the shopkeepers did during siesta in the city–Edwin grudgingly allowed it but made them work till suppertime to make it up. At dinner in the cafeteria Edwin surveyed the heads and shoulders drooped from the day.

"Hot day today, yes?" he asked. "Hot as any we've had. It's tough, days like this."

The young men nodded as one.

"Anybody have a story to tell from today's travels?"

When no one spoke up, Edwin frowned.

"All right, then," he said finally. "Let's bless the food we're about to eat. No, wait. Let me say one more thing."

He scanned the room, fixing his eyes briefly on each missionary. "You're here as boys doing the work of men in a hard place. For most of you, this is the one Mormon mission of your life. Some of you can't wait to get back home to mom's cookin' or the backyard pool. And I don't mind telling you, boys, I miss those things too.

"But for now, I want you to face the day as sunflowers. Don't wither, boys. Make a difference out there.

"Tomorrow, I want to hear a story or two from you. Let us pray."

CHAPTER 9

"You Tricked Me"

Red, naked in bed with his wives on either side, felt energized, as though he'd conquered the day. The adoption agency rep met him in San Francisco Javier de Satevo, a tiny village halfway between El Paso and Durango, took possession of the abandoned baby and counterfeit birth certificate from Teresa Cortez and handed Red $1,500 in cash. A good day's work. In the morning, he would pay Teresa and discuss a plan for the future. He felt good despite the heat and looked for clues in the ceiling cracks for a roadmap to sleepiness.

Then he felt her. Sam, lying on her side beside him, lazily traced her fingers along his naked leg, like a spider walking. He smiled, closed his eyes, and felt his manhood twitch. He leaned his head toward hers and they kissed. In the faint glow of a moon peering in through an open window, her hand found him and brought him fully to life. He rolled to face her and waited for a signal. He found it in her eyes, which betrayed a lusty urgency. He moved atop her and pushed two fingers inside. She moaned and arched her hips. He replaced his fingers with his hardness, locking his arms at the elbows above her to gain full entry. He relished the oozy glove sucking him inside and glanced at Del lying naked on her stomach. She was watching them. Emboldened, he moved his right arm down Del's back to her buttocks. She let him play while he fucked Sam, who writhed beneath Red. His senses were afire; temples throbbing, the musty scent of Sam's sex filling his nostrils and her minx-like mewing in his ears. Just then, Del slid over, sucked Sam's earlobe into her mouth and looked up at Red, who stared in wide-eyed amazement.

"What the Hell!" Red said. "What have you two been doin?"

Still gluing her eyes on Red's, Del smiled, turned Sam's face to hers, hungrily kissed her lips and slipped her tongue inside. She scooted closer, massaging Sam's smallish breasts with her hand, flicking each nipple between her fingers.

Red began churning his hips with abandon, overcome with the erotic movie playing out in his bedroom. Beads of sweat dripped from his forehead onto Sam, who already glistened and was gnawing passionately at Del's lips. Fearful of an unwanted pregnancy, Red was about to withdraw as the tremors of orgasm swam up his legs toward his crotch. That's when Del moved her hand from Sam's breasts to Red's butt and pressed him against Sam. He grunted as though she had cut him. Sam, already feeling orgasm overtake her, squealed like a pup, and dragged her nails across Red's back as he poured his essence into her and then, overcome, fell upon her. Heaving above her, the sweat they'd generated made squishing noises with the rise and fall of his chest. Del chuckled at the sound. All of them did.

"Man, that was somethin'," Red said finally, rolling off Sam. "Didn't know you two were so friendly, if you know what I mean."

"I 'spect there's a lot you don't know," Del said. She had pulled up the sheet to cover her nakedness.

"Such as?" he asked.

"Did you know Sam and I cried all morning after you took that baby girl away from here?"

Feigning indifference, Red replied, "I 'spect I did."

"Well Mr. Sterling Pierce, I 'spect you didn't know at all, or didn't care. I 'spect you didn't know Sam here is ovulatin' right now neither."

Red eyed Sam, who'd rolled on her stomach with her legs and eyes tightly closed. On her face was a blissful smile.

"So that's it, huh? You tricked me!"

"Weren't no trick at all, Red," Del said. "Sam wants her own baby and I do too. Best thing for you to do is keep goin' along. It's high time we were a family!"

Red rolled onto his side facing Sam. Best to clam up and sleep, he decided, and sleep he did, like a baby.

Red pulled the bishop aside after services the following Sunday and told him he'd given Baby Esmerelda to an adoption agency. "My wives are mighty angry about it, to tell ya' the truth," he'd said, "but it'll pass. Didya make those calls to the bishops?"

"I did," Edwin said. "Meet me in my office and I'll give you a couple names the agency can call."

Before the first summer was over, two more newborns appeared from nowhere at the makeshift Mormon church. One in July; the other August. Red's wives took charge and when no one stepped up to claim them, Red was cleared to fix it. In his August dispatch to Mormon elders in Salt Lake City, the bishop recounted the proceedings, adding:

"Only the most desperate of women would abandon a child. The barrios of this city are full of such women—wombs bulging, bellies empty. They scrounge for cornmeal and beans and there's always lots of mouths to feed. Many, many husbands have migrated to work in the States. Some are arrested and others never come back. Orphanages in Mexico are terrible places where children are warehoused. My heart aches for these children and their mothers.

"I believe we're doing an important service as a church by uniting orphaned children with childless families in the States. My fellow bishops in Provo have been encouraged by the amount of interest from ward families there. These adoptions, I think, are a blessing for all involved, especially the children.

"We've only scratched the surface of this need. What could be accomplished if we offered adoption counseling in the barrios? My missionaries could spread the word throughout the city. Perhaps LDS Family Services in Utah could help coordinate a plan?

"I look forward to your guidance on expanding our outreach in Durango."

In a week Edwin Youngblood's office phone rang.

"Bishop Youngblood, this is Evan Ralston in Provo. I'm head of international outreach for the Church. Your latest dispatch was passed along to me.

"In a few days you're going to receive an official response from me via letter. I'm afraid you may not find it very encouraging," he said.

Edwin braced for a lecture. "Let me guess. It's a no to the adoptions."

"Well, now that's the reason for my call, Brother," Ralston said. "We think your efforts to help these abandoned children are laudable. We fully support bringing adoptive children into our Church universe. When a Mormon couple adopts a child, that child can be sealed in the temple to the eternal family.

"But . . ." Edwin said.

"But you'll get no sanction for your efforts from the Church."

"Why not?"

"It's because the only international adoptions Mexico recognizes are the ones approved by the government through its orphanages. It takes years and they won't allow adoptions of newborns. As a Church with outreach programs in Mexico, our position must mirror that of the government. That's what the letter will say.

"What it won't say is what you already know, that dozens of private adoption agencies along both sides of the border fly under the government's radar. The government pretty much ignores them and so do we.

"So where does that leave me?" Edwin asked.

"It leaves you up to your own devices," Ralston said. "You might want to get a radar gun."

Edwin frowned. "That's Church humor, right?"

"My own, I'm afraid," Ralston said.

"So officially, I don't have your blessing but unofficially, I do?"

"Let me put it another way," Ralston said. "The Church supports legitimate adoptions. They help us grow the Mormon congregation. That's our stance."

Edwin was silent for a moment, then said, "I have a few empty classrooms here. We could set up a counseling center. Adoption would be just one of many options for these unwed mothers to consider."

"There's an idea!" Ralston said. "Keep me posted on how things work out! On another note, the plans for the permanent mission are going well. We should have blueprints to you within a month or two."

CHAPTER 10

2002 - THE REUNION

In the barrios of Mexico's interior, time idles like a sidetracked boxcar. Electricity had come to Rosa's neighborhood in the early 1980s, but Calle Rubio was still unpaved; the dusty jalopies of yesteryear more abundant beside it than working ones.

Hers was the northernmost dwelling in a string of seven clustered between a dry creek bed and a sloping hill. Hundreds of others dotted the barrio in similar pockets; a dozen here, fifteen there, and went on for a mile or more in all directions. Some of the dwellings were splashed with color. Most were like Rosa's; the color of the earth, bleached and hardened to a light adobe brown. Had there been money enough, her casucha would have been orange, as it was a notion when Rosa first married to paint her home the color of the Mexican Hat flower.

Only once did Rosa have money for luxuries such as paint. That was when Teresa Cortez had come for baby Ruben. The Durango midwife had given her 6,200 pesos, the equivalent of $450 U.S. dollars, that she placed in a *stack on Rosa's sleeping mat where Ruben was resting. The midwife picked up the baby, gently loosened his swaddling and examined him, noting with interest how Rosa had cut the umbilical cord and clamped it with a clothes pin. Ten toes. Ten fingers. The midwife's lips curled into a half smile.*

"He will be a handsome man," she had said in Spanish. "I will find this one a good Catholic home."

Rosa, still weak from childbirth, signed a paper Teresa gave her relinquishing her parental rights and watched wordlessly as the midwife rewrapped the child and left.

Though she could have painted a rainbow on her adobe walls then Rosa had not touched the money for a month. When she looked on the stack of bills emblazoned with the faces of dead Mexican presidents, she saw Ruben instead, puffy-eyed and swollen, cradled in the arms of a stranger.

Rosa decided she would spend the late afternoon with a good sweeping of her home. She had spent the day braiding colored wool that would eventually become a serape blanket. It was the time of year, in summer, when the deadly white scorpion, indigenous to the Durango region, was most active. The creatures commanded the full respect of the villagers, especially Rosa, whose husband died in agony from the sting of one after he fell drunk in a rut by the road when she was only twenty-two. Authorities told her that when found his left shoulder was partially buried in the mud while the scorpion that killed him stood atop his right shoulder, taunting them.

The floor of Rosa's hut was earthen, packed hard and smooth by use. The sweeping did not take long though she took care in the corners and around her furniture to watch for scorpions. There was little to hide behind. She had a straw mat for sleeping, two handmade stools of cow hide and wood, an old trunk given to her by Lomas, her son, and a card table in the center of the hut. A crude fireplace and a large water basin with a hunk of cardboard as a cover were centered along one wall, with a metate grinding stone she used to make tortillas. The trunk, where she kept her weaving utensils and wool, was an ugly brown, its skin peeled away. The brass edgings were blackish. Rosa took care to clear the dust from it with her broom and then wiped it down.

She wore the clothes she had slept in the night before and the night before that. Each morning when she rose from her mat, she modestly smoothed down the wrinkles from her cotton dress and after washing her thin face from the basin, she was ready for the day. On occasion, she would rummage through her trunk and retrieve a handheld mirror. She rarely liked what she saw. Years of sun exposure had baked her skin to a dark and leathery hide. It was dry and loose against her cheekbones, wrinkled along the forehead, under her eyes and along her neck. In America, she would have been mistaken for a woman of sixty instead of forty-six but in Durango, she looked like most other Mexican women her age. Nor did her bony frame set her apart. What little she made on blanket-making afforded her enough ground corn and flour to make tortillas but not always enough for beans to fill them. Her arms were long and thin as sapling branches, her legs weak; the left one twisted slightly, making her limp. But she was a clean woman. She sponged her body each evening and every third day, she washed her clothes by hand.

In front of the Mercado on the eastern fringe of Durango, only a handful of cars were in the parking lot but inside the market was bustling with women. Ruben went in for directions after noticing the pavement ended just beyond. Back in the car, he and Rebecca watched as the women came and went; some barefoot and many with a child carried papoose-fashion in a shawl. Except for the teenagers, who sported jeans, the women wore plain Mexican dresses or fluffy blouses with colorful skirts that reached their ankles.

"They dress conservatively," Rebecca noted. "Like Mormons do."

"I'm thinking we're within three miles," Ruben said. "Exciting, huh?"

"Dirt roads ahead," she said. "Not excited about that."

Rosa stood in her yard, knocking the dust from her broom. She sniffed the air and decided it smelled of a coming rain. Clouds were building to the west. She smiled at the thought of a cool down. Down the hill, on a distant street, she noticed a young man with his head leaning out the window of a blue car. He was talking to a local there. As she watched, the car turned around and disappeared. She saw it again minutes later on the road just beyond her own, creeping along, its brake lights strobing on and off. Few vehicles ventured so deeply into the barrio, and Rosa thought it odd. They must be very lost, she told herself.

Leaning against the broom, Rosa watched the car edge closer, closer still, until it stopped in front of her. The driver got out of the car and walked toward her. In his shorts and sandals, she could tell he was a tourista.

"Buenos dias, senora," Ruben said in perfect Spanish. He told her he was looking for 165 Rubio Street.

"Esta es Calle Rubio," Rosa replied, waving her arm back and forth at the road they were on. She knew nothing of street numbers for the ramshackle houses there. "Who do you seek?" she asked in Spanish.

"Rosa Ramon Segovia," he replied.

Rosa took a step backward and eyed the stranger fearfully. Her mind raced but took her nowhere. *I do not know this man,* she told herself. *Why would he come looking for me?*

"Do I know you?" she asked. Her eyes narrowed. "Yo soy Rosa Segovia."

"Oh, I . . ." Ruben stammered, his smile melting into the gape of surprise. Adrenalin rushed to his brain: *Have I found her? So quickly? Say something,* Ruben told himself. He blurted it out. "I uh . . . um . . . I am your son," he said finally, forgetting his Spanish. "Yo soy su hijo. Yo soy Ruben."

Faint thunder rumbled in the distance, but Rosa was struck as if by lightning. A darkness clouded her sight, her eyelids flickered up and down and her grip on the broom went slack. Before Ruben could reach her, she spun like a dying dust devil to the ground.

When the darkness lifted, Rosa found herself lying on her mat in her casucha; Ruben on his knees beside her, fanning her with his hat and offering bottled water from the car. His eyes were full of tears. Rebecca stood in the doorway, where two neighbors stood outside speaking in hushed, excited tones.

Rosa sipped the water and tried to regain her bearings. Outside, rain was coming to chase away the neighbors.

Ruben's face came into view. The harsh light of the naked lightbulb above cast him in a halo; light radiated from his hair, but his face was in shadow. Rosa thought for a moment he was an angel. She rummaged her mind for some clue from the past, some mole or birthmark; some proof of nature that would assure her this angel could be her Ruben. She could not remember one.

He spoke to her in Spanish. "Please forgive me for coming here like this. I tried to write many times. Do you get mail here?"

She shook her head no. "No one comes here," she said, "except my Lomas."

"This Lomas, he is your other son?" Ruben asked. A childlike grin creased his face at the notion of a brother unknown to him.

Rosa nodded and wiped her eyes. Modestly pushing at her dress as she rose, she walked unsteadily to one of her stools. Ruben noticed she had a slight limp. She sat upright, hands in her lap, head drooped and did not look upon her guest. She stared instead at her dress and found herself disgusted with it; the food stains here and there she hadn't noticed before, the frayed edges.

Ruben frowned then, surprised how she seemed suddenly to be shrinking from him. He had anticipated the reunion would be more bittersweet than bitter, perhaps even festive. Instead, she was withdrawn.

He surveyed the one-room structure. "This," he said softly to himself in English, "is what I saw when I came into the world." He placed his fingers against a wall of clay and straw. The walls were crude but strong, fired through the years by the heat of the Mexican sun and inside, by the fireplace. "It's not what I imagined."

"Que?" Rosa asked. She spoke no English.

Ruben rose and pulled a stool near her. He told her how he found her using adoption papers and promised to show them to her. He told of growing up in Utah the son of a respected Mormon elder and bishop, of his two-year stint as a Mormon missionary in Albuquerque and of his marriage to Rebecca. He told her she had a granddaughter and fumbled for her picture in his wallet. Rosa smiled at the photograph then pushed it away.

"Why have you come here?" she said, her voice quavering. She glanced toward Rebecca, who was staring aghast at Rosa's cooking station, with its brass pot on a hook in the fireplace and two small pans on the rocks beside it.

"I don't understand," Ruben said.

"You were my son for two days. Now you belong to someone else." Salty tears welled in her eyes again.

"You are my mother," Ruben said softly.

"I only bore you. Then I sold you like a calf at the market." She returned her hands to her face and, bracing her elbows on her legs, wept hard. Twenty-five years of regret and guilt poured into her hands.

Ruben closed his eyes and for the briefest moment, regretted coming to Durango. He knew such things happened in third-world countries. Money greased many palms. His dream the night before was a perversion of that.

He watched her for a long time and when she composed herself, he took her hands in his and looked into her pained face.

"You had your reasons for what you did," Ruben said. "You are my mother and it's important you know that I'm happy. I have a good life. A family. The adoption was a blessing. That's what I came to tell you."

Above them the slackening rain pinged at the sheet-metal roof. Her eyes darted to his. He opened his arms and she fell into them.

"You are wanting to know of your father, yes?" Rosa said after a time.

"Is he alive?"

"Not to me," she said flatly. The rain outside had passed and the air was cool and pleasant. Rosa sucked it in. When she was ready, she explained how she was married at eighteen to a laborer five years her senior; how though it was not an arranged marriage, her parents received a cage of chickens for their blessing; how she moved in with her husband, Jesus Arredondo, in the casucha he had built.

"This one," she said, tracing Jesus' handiwork with her eyes. She told how a midwife helped her bring Lomas into the world. "Over there," she said, pointing to the mat. And she told how Jesus' death when Lomas was three had brought intense poverty upon the household.

"He loved his tequila too much anyway," she said. "There was never money for us."

"But your father, I think, was no drinker. He was just an evil man" she said. "Jose Sanchez, the rapist." She spat on the ground.

She told how Sanchez owned the grist mill nearby. He was a man of substance and Rosa had gone to him seeking work, but he propositioned her instead, offering a month's worth of cornmeal if she would lie with him. He was unapologetic and not the first; other men from the barrio made crude advances on the petite Hispanic widower in the year following her husband's death. Most smelled of liquor and sweat. None got past her door.

But one late summer day, she said, a young boy she did not know had knocked on her door. He told Rosa the grist mill owner sent him to tell her he might have work for her. He would expect her to visit him at the grist mill that evening to discuss it. She couldn't say no.

"I washed myself, combed my hair and put on a fresh dress," Rosa said, simply. "And I went."

The grist mill was less than a half mile from her casucha. Sanchez, a stocky man with strong arms who made a good living grinding corn, took her to the back of the mill to a small office. There was a bed there as well. On the bed was a basket containing bags of cornmeal, pinto beans, and a long coil of dried chorizo.

"I knew when I saw the food there was no job for me," Rosa said solemnly. "But I knew also I wouldn't be leaving without that food." It was over in minutes, she said. The next day, Lomas and Rosa ate till their bellies were full. A month later Rosa realized she was pregnant.

"I hated this man. He was foul mouthed and rough," she said to Ruben. "I had no wish to have his baby."

Rosa cast her eyes skyward, as she had done the night Jose Sanchez pushed her dress to her shoulders and used his knees to force himself between her legs. She had asked for God's forgiveness then and now, as she sat before Ruben and made her confession, she tried to imagine the clang of a Catholic church bell somewhere out of earshot tolling forgiveness. Though she was hardly a devout Catholic and rarely went to services, Rosa kept a rosary in her trunk and knew most of the prayers by heart.

She told Ruben of finding a midwife with connections

to a Juarez adoption agency that placed babies with childless American couples and offered birth mothers a "gift" of money for their sacrifice. She went to the Catholic mission at the edge of the barrio and asked a priest for guidance. "He told me the government would not want me to do this; that adoptions outside of Mexico were discouraged." But he said the church would not condemn it if the adopting parents were Catholic.

"The midwife promised she would put you with a Catholic family," Rosa said. "But you said you are a Mormon."

"Mormons are a lot like Catholics," Ruben replied.

"You believe in the same God Catholics do?"

"We believe in God and families and doing what's right in God's eyes, like Catholics," Ruben responded. "Mormons have missions in Mexico and around the world, like Catholics. We have no priests or confessionals, but we have bishops and we pray to the same God."

Rosa was silent for a time. "Do Mormons have something to do with ladders? There was a sign at the clinic where I met Teresa. It said ladder saints or something."

"Latter Day Saints," Ruben corrected.

"I do not know of Mormons," she said then. "I have prayed for you many times. Your face haunted my thoughts long after you were born. I see the face of a man now. It is a good face."

CHAPTER 11

1974 – ALABASTER ANNIE

In the great room of his ranch house, Eduard Marmoles awaited Red's arrival sunk into his favorite armchair. Though still midmorning, he nursed a bourbon, idly swirling the lone ice cube between sips. His free hand swept back dyed coal hair that hung like tangly mop strands. He had on a favorite Western shirt, black with pearl buttons and a stiff, reinforced collar, black jeans, and polished black and chestnut brown dress boots. He liked to look good but was lazy about it; he found the cut of fine clothes an ego boost and had a maid press and pick them daily. But Eduard, who viewed grooming as a nuisance since he tolerated so few visitors, didn't mind how his nose hairs flared and rarely bothered shaving until it made his face itch. Red, of course, didn't qualify as a visitor. He was strictly a hired hand.

At the gate of the 400-acre ranch of mostly cactus and mesquite, Red fumbled with the combination. He never knew if it would be 1926 or 1962. Red assumed they were dates of some import and Marmoles changed the combination often. This time, 1926 got him in.

From the gate, the ranch house was hidden. The road winded and until it crested to reveal a low valley shielded by an oval of scrub oaks, the walled hacienda beyond was elusive; its earthy hue blending with the soil. A cattle guard at the entrance jostled Red's car over the spaced piping, jarring the steering wheel in his hands. Inside, freshly mown grass beside the paved driveway wrapped the home itself in a carpet of green like a desert oasis. A gardener tending flowers bordering the property's wide veranda waved a greeting to Red, who nodded and stepped briskly to the front door of polished mesquite, where a uniformed maid motioned for him to clean his boots on the welcome mat before ushering him in.

"Howdy, Mr. Marmoles." Red sauntered toward his host, who extended his hand to him. "Thanks for seein' me today." The eyes of a dozen mounted animals on the high adobe walls followed Red as he strode past oversized Mexican furniture of wood and ornamental iron suspended above the dark terrazzo floor by seven rugs.

"Always good to be seen," Marmoles said, grinning. "Have a seat. I take it you've got something on your mind."

"Fall's comin' at us kinda fast this year, ain't it?" Red said as he took a chair. He watched the caramel-colored liquid slosh in the attorney's glass.

Marmoles smiled. "I guess you wouldn't mind one of these. Help yourself. Booze is over there." He pointed to the bar topped with a decanter, glasses, and an ice bucket in a corner of the large room with high ceilings crisscrossed by cedar beams. A fourteen-point white-tailed buck's head hovered over the bar.

Red admired the animal, idly took a sip, and smiled.

The booze was well aged and smooth.

"This is better than fine," he said. He turned back to Marmoles.

"Your idea of bringing a midwife into the picture for those adoptions was a good one," Red began. "The adoption rep told me point blank those birth certificates would do the trick. I don't think he cared a lick if they were phony."

"Phony's not a word I would use," Marmoles admonished. "I would characterize them as perfectly legitimate birth certificates signed by a legitimate, licensed midwife for the state of Durango."

"She's a help fer sure," Red said of Teresa Cortez. "Money well spent."

"You going to get to the point sometime soon?" Marmoles asked, rising from his chair, and crossing the room to place his empty glass on the bar. "I've got some legal work to tend to." He looked at his watch.

Red finished his own drink. "Here's the deal. Bishop Youngblood's of a mind to do counseling services and prenatal care for pregnant women in the schoolhouse we use."

"Well, now, that's very industrious of him," Marmoles said. "Did you plant that seed?"

"I coulda," said Red. "I laid it on thick how lucky them orphaned babies were to be growin' up in the States 'stead of some barrio."

"Indeed they are," the attorney said. He walked to his desk, fished out a legal pad and, returning to his chair, began making notes.

"So I was thinkin' we get Cortez involved, coachin' these women about adoption," said Red. "Ya know, plant some seeds, like you said." He looked at Marmoles and saw he was smiling.

"It's a fine idea, Red," Marmoles said. "If these women get prenatal care, the odds of them having healthy babies goes way up. And with a church behind it, there'll be lots of interest. Hmmmm."

"And maybe some more babies come our way," Red said.

"Like chicks in an incubator," Marmoles said finally.

Marmoles scribbled notes in silence while Red's eyes roamed the room. A javelina with yellowed tusks, propped above a marble pedestal by medal rods, sneered from one corner. Other stuffed animals indigenous to the region were scattered about, including a bobcat, a coyote, and a turkey with flared tail feathers. Red presumed they were trophies.

"You must do a lot of huntin'," Red said.

"Nope. Ranch hands killed all of these. Had 'em stuffed for decoration. I like dead animals more than live ones, mostly."

"What about them rattlers?" Red asked, pointing to the glass encased terrarium along a side wall.

"They're alive. Couple of old timers, like me. I like to watch 'em eat mice," he said without looking up from his notepad. "I coulda filled a dump truck with rattlesnakes when I first moved out to this place."

The attorney put his pad down and walked back to the bar, where he poured another round for Red and himself.

"Have a seat, Red," he said. "It's time we talked of bigger things."

Red slouched with his drink in a chair beside a large round coffee table in the room's center. Marmoles sat across from him.

"When I helped you connect that first abandoned baby with an adoption agency, I really didn't give much thought to it," the attorney said. "You've been a good hand when it comes to my business dealings and I've come to trust the way you carry yourself. So I was happy to help."

"And I sure appreciate it, Mr. Marmoles," Red said, smiling.

"And now you've shown me something else. You've shown me you've got a real eye for opportunity," he continued. "I've been waiting a while for another one to come along. But now it has.

"You ever wonder why I use two different combinations on my gate lock?"

"Important dates, I figure."

"Correct. Now 1926 is the year I was born and 1962 is the year I got disbarred from practicing law in New York. Feds accused me of laundering money for the mob," he said, casting a distracted eye to his gardener watering flowers outside the room's full-length windows. "I wasn't. The mob paid me to buy off judges and police officials in the Big Apple. They couldn't track all the cash so they said I laundered it through my law firm.

"I was indicted but the case kinda fell apart and charges were dropped without a trial," he went on. "Nobody on the inside talked. State bar booted me out anyway, of course."

When he turned back to Red, Marmoles' eyes blazed with purpose. They bore down on the Tennessean like the business end of a shotgun. Red sat still as a tree trunk.

"Fact is, my name's not Marmoles. It's Zimmerman. Gene Zimmerman," he said calmly. "You should look it up.

I was a big-time wheeler dealer back then so it was quite the scandal."

Red took a big swig of his smoky booze. "Um, why are you telling me this, uh, Mr. Zimmerman?"

"Call me Marmoles. Zimmerman's dead and gone. I'm telling you because there're two kinds of people in this world. There're ones who need a fix and ones who do the fixing. I fixed things for people in New York for many years. Got rich doin' it. Now you're gonna be a fixer here in Mexico. You've already shown a real knack for it.

"I'm also telling you this because it looks like we're going to be partners. You're going to head up an adoption operation with the help of your ambitious young bishop."

"Whoa there!" Red stammered. "I'm gonna what?"

"You're going into the black market, Red. You're gonna sell babies. Big money in that," he said. "I'll finance the operation but strictly as a silent partner. We'll need your midwife in the mix too. Let's talk more while I show you the rest of the house."

Red stood uneasily and his right eye began to blink involuntarily. He rubbed it vigorously.

"I can see you're nervous, Red," the attorney said. "Don't be. This'll be slick as Vaseline. You'll see."

The two men's boots clicked on the tile floor as Marmoles led them to the kitchen, where spotless appliances of stainless steel blazed under fluorescent lighting. A wide cutting board island teemed with fresh vegetables awaiting the knife of Carmelita, the cook, who was busy washing dishes.

"Hola Carmelita," Marmoles chirped.

"Oh, hola Senor Marmoles!" she replied, turning to face the two men.

"Doesn't speak a word of English," he said to Red as they passed. "Wish my Spanish was better."

"Anyway, over there is the pantry and the butler's nook leading to the formal dining room," he said. "The table is mesquite. Beautiful, isn't it?"

"I'll say," marveled Red, admiring the orange and red hues of it. It was thick and marbled like a slab of bacon but varnished to a glasslike consistency. Brightly colored upholstery on the matching chairs, as though painted with broad brush strokes by a daring artist, complemented the woodwork.

In the hallway separating the dining and living rooms, Marmoles motioned to a painting illuminated by a ceiling light. "My first wife Annie. Alabaster Annie, I called her. An actress of sorts, commercials mostly."

Red leaned in. The portrait was a nude of a lithe young woman's backside. She was on a couch, looking over her shoulder at Red. He blushed.

Marmoles chuckled. "Yeah, most guys do the same thing. Hardly notice her face, that is."

"She's mighty fine, Mr. Marmoles, I'll say that!"

"In my study, I have photographs of my second and third wives," he said. "They were pretty, too. I was a sucker for the lookers. But women tend to tire of me and I of them.

"One thing I don't tire of is law books," he said, sliding open the doors to his study. "There's no better mistress than the law, Red. And the law on international adoptions is murky. Downright oozy."

Unlike other rooms in the house, the study was a cluttered mess. Books competed for floor space in happenstance piles, dangling like dominoes, rising like anthills. Catalogued law books filled bookcases that rose to the ceiling on three sides. Notepads with scribbled writing on them were strewn across the attorney's mahogany desk. Strips of paper used as hurried bookmarkers hung like confetti from the piles.

Red stepped gingerly into the room, which stank of cigar smoke. Marmoles opened a humidor at the end of his desk and pulled out two Cuban cigars. He clipped the tips off and handed one to Red, saying, "It's okay to smoke in here." Red accepted it greedily and held it in his stubby fingers, waiting for Marmoles to light his own. They puffed them to life and Red lifted two law books from a chair and sat while the attorney flipped a switch on his desk, turning on a window fan to suck out the smoke.

"I did some research on the rights of a newborn in Mexico before advising you on what to do with that first orphan baby," the attorney said. "Newborns don't have any.

"The rights belong to the father if he's in the household. Barring that, the mother decides. Barring that, it's a custody dispute. And in any dispute, the person with custody holds the hot hand. You've heard the phrase 'Possession is nine-tenths of the law?' Well, that's more or less the way things worked with those three adoptions you helped with."

Marmoles savored his cigar and pushed an ashtray toward Red. "So, there was no real liability on the part of your bishop. Youngblood, is it?"

"Yessir," said Red, flicking his cigar over the ashtray with care.

"Now the adoption agency took some risk on those deals because they didn't have something from the mothers relinquishing their parental rights," he went on. "They probably phonied something up for the adoptive parents, I imagine. But we won't have to worry about any of that from here on out. We're gonna set up our own adoption agency and we'll pay these expectant mothers to sign their parental rights to us. Then we'll have your midwife sign the birth certificates and we can fetch top dollar for them stateside," he said. "And the best part is . . . Do you know what the best part is, Red?" Marmoles said between puffs.

"Um, we get rich?" Red asked.

"It'll all be done with the blessing of the Mormon Church."

"I don't know about that part, Mr. Marmoles," Red chimed in. "Bishop Youngblood's a straight arrow. He won't cotton to payin' women for their babies. No way."

"Red, he doesn't need to know about that now, does he?"

"No. I guess he don't." Red looked confused again.

"Lemme back up a few steps, Red. I'm going too fast for you, I think. Your bishop wants to start a prenatal clinic for unwed mothers-to-be, right?"

"Right."

"So we put your midwife in charge of his little clinic and she cozies up to them and promises them cash money to give up a baby they don't even want in the first place," he said. "We let the church pay for their medicines and meals. The Church fattens them up, if you will, then when they're due we take them to Juarez, or El Paso, where they have the babies.

"And we hook 'em up with Mormon families in Utah who think the whole thing's sanctioned by their church," he said. "Nobody asks any questions."

Marmoles leaned back in his chair and with a self-satisfied grin, sucked in a big puff of smoke and let it drift slowly outward, obscuring his face.

"It's clean, Red," he continued, "and except for the money we give the mothers, it's legit. The babies become our property and we charge what the market will bear. And that's somewhere between fifteen and twenty thousand dollars apiece!"

"What? You're kiddin' me, right?" Red asked, stunned.

"I don't kid about business, Red."

"So what's my role?"

"Start by getting Cortez on board. Offer her $2,000 plus expenses for every healthy baby she births. Tell her if she brings us a baby on the side, through her regular midwife work in the barrios, we give her more, say $3,000," he said. "Are you an elder in your church ward?"

"Don't think I'm elder material, Mr. Marmoles."

"Of course you are. Youngblood already trusts you. On the inside, you'll have his ear."

CHAPTER 12

A PLAN HATCHED

Edwin convened the elders after services that Sunday. There were six of them besides Edwin and as they waited for the cafeteria to empty of parishioners Brother Michael Jones, a chatty expatriate with dyed brown hair, joked how his bad Spanish got him in trouble at the flea market a few days before.

"I was there with Dottie and noticed a pinata shaped like a duck laying on a blanket in front of this pretty young senorita," he said. "It was unique, and I thought about it for my grandson's birthday. But the duck's bill was kinda long and raggedy, so I say 'te ves gracioso pero me gusta,' which I thought meant 'it looks funny, but I like it.' She looks at me all surprised and starts to tear up. Then her brother notices and he comes over and he wants me to explain why I told her 'you look funny but I like you.'"

The men roared with laughter.

"Sensitive, these Mexican women. Dottie bailed me out before I got my butt whipped," Michael finished. "I think she told them I was some kind of doofus."

The bishop passed out copies of his August dispatch to Utah, conveyed his conversation with Brother Ralston and read the formal response Ralston sent. He outlined his idea to offer pregnancy services to the community at large; counseling, prenatal midwifery.

"It's a way to show Durango that Mormons care about them," said the bishop.

"Who's gonna run it?" asked Simon Slaughter, an expat with rural roots in Idaho.

"I haven't worked that part out yet," said the bishop. "The key will be finding a good midwife who'll do the prenatal care. I think I can oversee it for a time and, of course, we should be able to count on ward members for help here and there."

"It's a good cause and all but it sounds to me like the Church ain't all that keen on this," Slaughter responded.

"I got the opposite feeling from talking with Brother Ralston, despite what he said in that letter," Edwin said. "He just wants to make sure that any adoptions that come out of this are legit.

"Those three orphans abandoned here were turned over to a reputable adoption agency in Juarez and they found Mormon families to place them with. I don't have any qualms about doing more of that, frankly. Especially after seeing the way the orphanages operate here in Mexico, right Brother Speck?"

John Speck removed his glasses, nodded, and took his cue to speak. "The bishop and I visited Durango's orphanage a few days ago. It's full of children without hope. You can see it in their eyes. They go as babies and they just never leave. The older ones were like zombies; walking around and all, but dead inside."

"Well said, John," Edwin said. "Really well said. And the babies; nobody held them, talked to them. I'm going back next month and hold as many as they'll let me."

"You'll have to do it without me!" said Brother Speck, shaking his head. "I ain't goin' back."

The elders voted on Edwin's plan with a show of hands. Red was tasked with finding a midwife to run the clinic.

"Got one ready to go," Red said over the phone.

Edwin took the phone from his ear and held it in front of his face. "How do you do that?" he said.

"Do what?" Red asked.

"How do you know what people need before they know it?"

"Name's Teresa Cortez, she's a top-notch midwife and a former registered nurse and she'll work fer cheap," Red said. "Anythin' else ya need?"

The bishop, stupefied, shook his head. "No," he said, finally. "But I'm sure you'll think of something."

Edwin made Red an elder the next day.

In time the church buzzed with activity. Missionaries were given new marching orders, pitching free prenatal care to women of the barrios. Elders set to work converting an empty classroom into a clinic with a tiny waiting area and two hospital beds separated by curtains. Medical gloves, a speculum, swabs, towels, and jellies were bought.

In a month, Edwin caught sight of a short husky woman in orange scrubs scurrying down the hall. Arms resting on her hips, she was inspecting activities in the clinic. Her dark hair was in a bun and a pair of glasses hung from her neck. She was scribbling something in a notebook.

"Are you with the city hospital," the bishop asked as he approached.

"No. I'm your midwife. Teresa Cortez," she said in Spanish, offering her hand, which Edwin promptly shook.

"Great. You're finally here," he said, being careful not to stare at the two dark moles on her face: one below her right eye and another staring back at him from her chin. With her caramel-colored skin, he immediately thought of giblets swimming in a bowl of gravy. "What a generous thing you're doing. Can't thank you enough."

Teresa had seen that look before. With a half-smile to Edwin, she turned her attention back to the clinic. The room was being painted bright white and fresh fluorescent light bulbs had been installed in the ceiling. "Might want to put some covers over those lights," she suggested, squinting. "Kinda bright, don't you think?"

"Hospital white, that was the thought," he said. "When the paint dries you can do what you like with it. Come, let's get to know each other." He waved her down the hall to his office, where she sat stiffly on the edge of her chair.

"So how do you know my favorite church brother, Sterling Pierce?" Edwin said brightly. "We all call him Red, you know."

"He heard of me from the locals. Was needing some advice on the baby left on your doorstep," she said.

"Ah, yes. Red's not shy about connecting with people, is he?"

"He is not," she said.

"Do you mind if I ask why you're doing this?" he asked.

She looked toward the draped office window, where a long slice of the afternoon sun slipped inside and drew a line of light across the bishop's desk. She watched the dust particles animate the air. "I was raped by my step-father as a child; many times," she said, fixing her eyes back on his. "I ran away when I was fifteen and with child.

"My daughter's a constant reminder of those times. It's not her fault, of course, but I treat her like it was," she confessed. "I keep seeing him in her. It would have been better, for her and me, if I'd given her to someone else to love."

In her eyes, Edwin detected little hint of emotion, no glint of remorse. It was an honest detachment, he thought, clear and steely.

"I'm very sorry for what you went through," the bishop responded. "If I may ask, are you Catholic?"

"I'm a bad Catholic," Cortez said.

"Married?"

"Never been. Never will be," she said bluntly. "You'll figure out soon enough I'm kind of a loner. I do my job and I go. Men mostly just get in my way."

Edwin was silent a moment. Her frankness was not beguiling. Still, he did not find it offensive. "Well, I guess we don't have to be the best of friends, Teresa. I won't interfere with your duties because I don't have time to. But you'll need to consult with some of the elders from time to time, including Red. Can you do that?"

"Of course," she replied. "Just don't ask me to marry any of them."

Edwin laughed. "You're in luck. Mormons don't do arranged marriages," he quipped.

There was no ribbon cutting. No ceremony. A simple sign saying "Prenatal Clinic" in Spanish with the hours 3 p.m. – 7 p.m. was posted on an exit door of the school's east wing. No one came the first couple weeks. Then three did. Then six.

Among the first were prostitutes from Durango's red-light district, cast out by pimps who saw no hypocrisy in it, though they surely played a role in the women's predicaments. In the world of promiscuity for profit, protruding bellies were bad for business.

Three of them showed up together one morning, lacking the courage to come alone. Isabela Herrera, a busty woman street-named "Angel," fidgeted in a tube top and cutoffs that fully exposed her outstretched belly. "Rose" Guerrero, in a skirt that barely covered her hips, was in her second trimester and beginning to swell. She nervously mauled a tuft of hair hanging off her shoulder. "Randi" Sifuentes, her hair bleached an orange blond and wearing a clingy, worn nightclub dress, looked no older than nineteen. Her nervous smile revealed two gold teeth.

They looked and smelled like the street urchins they were: earthy, boozy, cigarette smoky. They practiced hypocrisy of a different sort; their malady was due in part to a Catholic ritualism so entrenched that even prostitutes considered abortion a sin and thus carried their babies to term; only to abandon them afterward to a relative or orphanage.

Teresa seized on their plight and urged the bishop to take them in, if only to supervise their prenatal care. A second classroom became a makeshift dormitory with sleeping mats and sheets hung as walls between them. A beat-up bus to shuttle the women to the free clinic downtown for shots and checkups was purchased. The residents ballooned to six as fall set in and marked time in lily-white Mexican pullovers of cotton with tiny flowers stitched on, a donation from a local vendor. The brothers and sisters of the ward brought in toiletries, pillows, magazines. Teresa Cortez ran it all like a military boot camp with mandatory exercise classes and regimented diets. The alcoholics were sent to rehab and the heroin addicts were shown the door; addicted mothers meant addicted babies.

On Sunday mornings, a back row of cafeteria chairs was reserved just for them. Attendance was a must. Rose, Randi, and Angel, invariably together, fidgeted as one; scratching private itches and glaring unapologetically at the Mormon men who snuck a curious or disapproving glance. "Eyes front" became the rallying cry of Mormon wives, on constant vigil with their men and children.

The bishop took it all in stride and to a wife who complained offered: "These women are clay for us to mold, Sister. Don't forget Mary Magdalene was a prostitute but now she has a pew in Heaven beside Jesus."

Red, surveying things one Sunday, remarked afterward to Edwin: "You remind me of a Pentecost preacher who came around here a few years back. He darn-near lived in the red-light district for a while, prayin' over whores and such. And he saved some fer sure I imagine. But when all that preachin' started scarin' customers away, the pimps paid the police to run him out of town."

"And your point?" Edwin queried.

"The game's fixed, Bishop. Some of these women make more money in one night than their customers make in a month. They may not like the work but they surely love the money."

"I'm not naïve," the bishop responded. "We're not

trying to rid the world of prostitution."

"Yessir. That's here to stay," said Red. "And that's what most of these women will most likely go back to."

"I know that, too," the bishop intoned. "But you won't mind if I try to save one or two in the meantime, do you?"

Red smiled, shook his head and crossed the room to shake Edwin's hand. "Do your darndest, Bishop," he said. "I counted nine women in church today needin' all the savin' you can give."

It was the beginning of what the locals came to call la incubadora.

Lines at the clinic grew longer. Pregnant barrio women began regular visits for exams and free vitamins. Many brought their children, who found cookies in the waiting area.

One day, Rosa Ramon Segovia took her place in line with her four-year-old son Lomas. It was a three mile walk to the clinic. Still in her first trimester and barely showing, she clutched a handkerchief in one hand to cover her mouth to fight off the nausea. Cortez could see she wasn't holding down food; fatigue drooped her shoulders, and her arms and legs were bony thin. She gave her over-the-counter medicine for the nausea and, finding her blood pressure elevated, scheduled a bus trip to the hospital district for a prescription. On Rosa's second visit, she confided the tale of the baby's father, the gristmill owner, and how he contrived his way with her.

"Do you not want this baby?" Cortez quizzed. With a stethoscope against Rosa's exposed belly, she listened for a heartbeat. It was strong and steady.

Rosa closed her eyes and said, softly, "God forgive me, no."

"No one could blame you for this," said the midwife. She leaned in, as if to whisper something in Rosa's ear but a clatter outside made her stop. She rose quickly to separate two women arguing with a third who had cut in line. When she returned, Rosa was sitting on the edge of the examining table. Tears rolled down her cheeks.

"I don't have time to talk anymore today," Teresa said. "But think about this. In America, many couples who cannot have children want to adopt babies. They have homes with toilets and kitchens and air conditioning. They live in neighborhoods with schools and parks and playgrounds.

"Give me your baby when it is born and I will find it a home. In return, you will receive 1,600 pesos, enough to feed you and your son for a year."

Rosa stared blankly at Cortez. "You can do all this?"

"I can and I will deliver your baby for free."

The young mother wiped her eyes with her handkerchief. "I will think on this," she said and rose to leave.

"Come back in a month," said the midwife. She turned away and in a loud voice ordered "Next!"

CHAPTER 13

2002 – DAY THREE

Rosa Segovia liked how the wind sped by when she rode in cars. In her twenties working as a maid, she tied her hair back with a rubber band and leaned her head out the window of the station wagon used to shuttle barrio women to affluent neighborhoods. It made her feel carefree as a child.

Rosa beamed when Ruben and Rebecca returned from their hotel and announced they should go for a ride. She tied her hair back and stuck her head out, first when they took her to the post office where, tucked in a mail slot marked "165" in a dusty back room, were a dozen letters from Ruben. A rubber band that once held them together was petrified and in pieces and the letter edges chewed away by rodents. Rosa wanted them anyway.

Ruben then searched out a hardware store to bring a taste of the 20th Century to Rosa's primitive world. He bought an extension cord, an electric fan, a can opener, Tupperware, ice trays, a portable refrigerator, and a large cooler. At the Mercado, he picked out fresh fruit and vegetables, canned staples, ice, beans, tortillas, skirt steak and Coca-Cola.

Finally, in a shop at a nearby market square, Rosa picked out a new dress in the colors of a rainbow, and she smiled into the wind on the way home.

Ruben inserted the extension cord into the electrical plug on the side of the light socket and let it dangle to the floor. He put the fan and refrigerator on the card table and plugged them in. They clicked, hummed, and whirred to life. He filled the cooler with ice, put the meat and vegetables inside it and the Cokes in the fridge. He told Rosa to leave the fridge on constantly and save the fan for the heat of the day.

"They will not use much electricity," he promised her.

Rosa said she was thankful but seemed more interested in the dress laid across her sleeping mat and the ragged letters she continued to clutch. The rest of the modern world to Rosa just seemed like so much noise.

She spent the remainder of the morning preparing lunch. She did not cook in the fireplace in summer but instead used a small pit outside and built a fire with fragrant mesquite wood. Over it she placed a grill fashioned from a piece of steel mesh that had once covered the bed of a pickup truck in a salvage yard. She rubbed the steak with oil, cumin, cayenne and salt and pepper, scooped the canned refried beans into a pot and, while the meat and beans cooked, made pico de gallo with onions, tomatoes, peppers and cilantro.

Ruben proclaimed the food delicious and ate three tortillas. Rosa's verdict: The store-bought tortillas and canned beans were a waste of good money; lacking the flavor of homemade.

"I will cook for you tonight," she announced. When Ruben reminded her they were visiting Lomas that evening, she shrugged and said, "Then I will cook for you there."

The visit would be a surprise since Rosa had no way to reach Lomas ahead of time. Usually, Lomas did the visiting since he had a bicycle he rode to work at a garment factory on the fringes of the city. Working twelve hour shifts in the warehouse since he was fourteen, Lomas rented a tidy three-room concrete block home with indoor plumbing, electricity, a television and a window-unit air conditioner.

That afternoon, Ruben put Rebecca on a plane back to Utah as previously planned. He returned and sat on the floor leaning against a wall of Rosa's simple house and watched her weave together wool threads to create a multi-colored blanket row. When she finished one, she began another, nimbly braiding a half dozen threads into something with ropelike strength. He noticed her knotted finger joints and thought the work painful, but her face showed no discomfort. And with the fan tunneling air between the open front and back doors, she looked quite serene, as if riding the wind again.

Occasionally a wasp buzzed around, but Rosa would wave it off with a lazy sweep of the broom. When a hungry chihuahua sniffed at the back door for scraps, she shooed him casually without interrupting her work. Flies were another matter. Two of them hovered over Ruben and dive-bombed his legs. He swatted and missed, over and again until Rosa, glancing over, suggested he try both hands. "Clap like this," she said, gesturing. Ruben did. It didn't work but when the flies tired of the game they flitted elsewhere.

Then Ruben sensed movement to his right. Shifting his gaze he saw a menacing scorpion marching toward him along the junction of the floor and wall. Leaping to his feet, he dispatched it with a sandal bottom. Thwack!

"Whoa," he exclaimed.

"I'm sorry," Rosa exclaimed, rising quickly. "That one, the white scorpion, is the kind that killed my husband." She sent Ruben outside so she could check for others. He returned bathed in sweat.

"Hot one," he said and sat nearer the fan on the other stool. Glancing nervously about for other marauders while wiping his forehead with his hand, it occurred to Ruben that the barrio would surely have killed him had he not been taken from it. The only question would be the manner of death, whether by scorpion, rattler, rabid dog, or simple heat stroke. He closed his eyes and said a silent prayer for the good fortune of his life.

Rosa, meanwhile, grappled with her superstitious nature. Was the scorpion's visit an omen? What God would snatch away her son a second time? She wondered this and promised herself to seek the counsel of her priest. Perhaps he would know what to make of it.

"I was trying to remember the last time I found a scorpion in my home" Rosa said aloud. "It has been years."

As the afternoon advanced to dusk, Rosa sent Ruben outside again so she could put on her new dress. She dug out her mirror, combed her shoulder-length hair and beckoned Ruben back.

"You look lovely," he said. Contrasted against her darkened skin, the dress was light and festive.

"Gracias," Rosa said. She was shuffling among her groceries. They loaded into Ruben's car a pot of raw pinto beans she'd been soaking, the remaining meat and some spices. Rosa was careful on the way to keep her head away from the window so as not to muss her hair.

The drive was short, mere minutes to Calle Juarez in a neighborhood similar to Rosa's. Smoke from a nearby meat packing plant hung in the air, its odor sour. The concrete exterior of the house was whitewashed but time had grayed it. Still, it had a cheery feel. Flowers in planters were arranged on the windowsills and native bushes grew beside the front door. A small dog yipped inside, prompting Lomas to open the door before Rosa could knock.

"Your brother has come," she said unceremoniously to Lomas as they hugged. He stared wide-eyed at Ruben behind her.

"Ruben?" he asked. "You are Ruben?"

"And you must be Lomas."

Rosa scurried inside to see her daughter-in-law and grandchildren. Lomas, wearing an untucked work shirt with a company name, Just Jeans, stitched on the front pocket, stood silent in the doorway, fumbling for words.

"Um, how did you find us?" he asked finally. He stepped forward and timidly extended his hand, as did Ruben, who stood a full head taller. Each studied the other's face.

Reaching into his back pocket, Ruben retrieved his adoption papers and offered them to Lomas. The original document, written in Spanish and stamped with Mexico's seal, authorized the adoption of Ruben Segovia to Edwin and Martha Youngblood, given to them by Rosa Ramon Segovia of 165 Calle Rubio, Durango in the state of Durango.

"We do not look like each other," Lomas said after examining the document.

"We had different fathers," Ruben reminded. "But I see our mother in you."

With high cheekbones and a thin, straight nose bridge, Lomas indeed favored his mother, Ruben noticed, and his ears were tucked against his head, as Rosa's were. His hair was swept back with just a slight hint of curl and he was thin and slightly lighter in pigment than his mother, but his shoulders were straight, not slumped, and Ruben noticed his grip was strong.

Ruben, too, had high cheekbones but a fatter nose with a faint hump in the middle, like an upside-down ski slope, and his chin was dimpled.

"Did you know my father, the grist mill owner?" Ruben asked.

"No. I never saw that awful man," he said. "When I was old enough to go beyond Calle Rubio, I went to the grist mill to throw rocks at it, but it was closed and empty. I don't know what happened to him.

"Come meet my family." Lomas gestured with his arm toward the door. Inside, the aroma of cooking already filled the house. Rosa and Emelia, Lomas' wife, moved about the tiny kitchen which had a countertop for chopping, a sink and a stove-top range. They were lost in conversation, though Emelia, wearing an apron over a simple Mexican dress, kept glancing curiously at Ruben, who smiled back sheepishly when he noticed. The kitchen opened to the main room, with walls of whitewashed concrete block, where the window air conditioner churned against the heat. The back of the house had a crude bathroom with a shower and toilet adjoining the only bedroom.

Two young boys in shorts and T-shirts sat cross-legged on the bare concrete floor with their noses inches from a small television screen dwarfed by a bulky wooden console enclosing it.

"Emelia, meet my long-lost brother," a smiling Lomas said, gesturing. Wiping her hands on her apron, Emelia walked briskly to Ruben and embraced him warmly. Then stepping back, she sized him up.

"You may be too good looking to be a Segovia," she teased, flashing a smile at Ruben and then her husband.

"Must be that dimple in your chin." Emilia hugged Ruben again and returned to the kitchen. Ruben liked Emelia immediately. She had a radiance about her, he thought, like someone from a higher station than the barrio.

Suddenly, the two boys were beside him.

"I'm Pablo," the five-year-old chirped, staring up at him. He looked to Ruben like his father in miniature.

"I'm very glad to meet you," Ruben said, smiling. Julio, three, was hugging Ruben's leg as if he'd known him all his life.

"Are you friends with my papa?" Pablo asked. He stuck out his hand for Ruben to shake.

Ruben extended his hand and Pablo gave it one exaggerated up and down movement. Ruben nodded his head amusedly, wondering from which television show the child had learned to shake hands. "Well, your father and I are brothers. I am your uncle."

Pablo frowned in confusion. "But Mama Rosa said you are from America?"

"He lives in America now. But he was born here,"

Lomas interjected. "He has been away a very long time so let's make him feel welcome."

"Julio, I think our guest would like his leg back," Emelia said.

Julio obliged, then tugged on Ruben's shorts for attention. "You're welcome," he said, smiling to reveal new teeth.

Dinner was a bowl of the most aromatic beans, peppers and spices Ruben could remember eating with carne asada, guacamole and homemade tortillas. For dessert, puffy sopapillas and honey. Talk was polite but brisk, with Pablo peppering Ruben with questions about life in America.

Ruben passed around a photo of Rebecca and Megan. Both were in Sunday dresses, posing on the front porch steps of their brick two-bedroom home in Provo. Lomas' boys ogled the swing suspended from chains on the Victorian style porch in the background. Lomas, when his turn came, studied the photo closely and Ruben noticed how his eyes darted from the picture to Rosa and back again. Ruben thought it mildly odd.

Afterward, Lomas suggested he and Ruben take a walk.

"When did you learn to speak Spanish? It is very good," Lomas asked. He had charted a course on the road toward a slope where dozens of patchwork homes were clustered. Most were primitive and darkly lit inside. Some had outhouses behind. A few had cactus stands in front as decoration.

"School. It was my main elective in high school, and I minored in it at college."

"You have a degree then?"

"In business, yes."

"You have done well," Lomas said. "I could see at dinner mother was fascinated by your stories about your life. It is hard to imagine such fine things you have seen and done."

Ruben sensed no hint of jealousy or bitterness in Lomas' remark. It came across as a simple observation. "I came here to tell your mother the same thing," he responded. "I am blessed that things turned out the way they did. Rosa did the right thing."

Lomas nodded and kicked at a rock in the street.

"I'm sure Rosa hasn't mentioned anything to you about your sister."

Ruben stopped walking. "What sister?" he asked.

Lomas faced Ruben. "I thought not. She never talks of it. Her memory of it is mostly gone now."

Lomas resumed walking. Ruben caught up but his eyes were riveted on him.

"About two years after you were adopted, our mom had another baby. There was this man who had taken an interest in her. I don't remember much of him except he was nice to her and me and came to visit off and on," Lomas said, pausing to wave casually to a man with a wide brimmed hat slipping past on a rusty bicycle. "He was a clean man, not a laborer like most men in the barrio. And she was lonely, I think.

"He took her out once or twice a month. Sometimes I went with them and sometimes I stayed home," he said. "I remember they talked some about being together, getting married."

Two dogs were fighting ahead of them. The racket was ferocious for several seconds until the loser, yelping in pain, ran under one of the houses to lick his wounds. Lomas watched with detachment.

"Anyway, she got pregnant and this man quit coming around. She hated him for that. After the baby came, the man came to see her. Mama made a fuss and wouldn't let him in," Lomas said. "That seemed to be the end of it but when the baby was three months old . . . her name was Maria . . . this man came back and took her while Mama was asleep. It was during the day and the doors were open because it was hot. I was at school, but Mama said she never heard a thing."

"He kidnapped Maria?" Ruben asked, incredulous. He paced as he listened, his face tight and angry. "Did anybody see him do it?"

"No one. But we all knew it was him. Who else would do such a thing?" Lomas asked.

"And no one saw Maria again?"

"No one. The police came. They took a report, but we had no photos to give them of the man or Maria. They said her kidnapping was the fifteenth that year in Durango; acted like it happened all the time," Lomas said. "They never did much of anything about it. In Mexico, you need money to get things done."

"I don't know what to say," Ruben said in a near whisper.

"It was a bad time," Lomas continued. "I remember Mama going door to door asking people if they'd seen her and screaming for her up and down the barrio. This went on for a month. Neighbors helped her make signs to put on trees, at the Mercado. She couldn't sleep. She didn't eat. She didn't cook. Neighbors brought us food...." Lomas' voice trailed off, his eyes downcast.

"Then one day she went to the police station and a detective told her they believed the man who took Maria was part of a smuggling ring," Lomas said. "They preyed on women of the barrio and stole their babies.

"She knew then that she had been deceived by this man from the beginning," Lomas said. "It did something to her mind. She couldn't remember her way home from the police station that day. An officer gave us a ride," he said. "When she awoke, she became frantic because Maria wasn't there. She had forgotten all about the kidnapping. It was like rats crawled in her head and ate at her brain. A doctor said she'd had a mild stroke."

They were back in front of Lomas' home. Ruben, leaning against the rental car door, pounded the fender with his fist. Is there no end to this woman's suffering, he wondered.

On the ride to Rosa's, Ruben brought up Maria. Rosa nodded as if expecting to be asked.

"I'm sorry I didn't tell you," she said. "Sometimes I remember things about that time, but mostly there is nothing there."

Her window was down, and she let the cooler air of evening wash her face. "I just get headaches when I try to remember," she said. "My priest, Father Guadalupe, said it was too much for me to bear so God worked like a spider to put cobwebs in my head . . . so the memory would die and I could live on."

"Yeah," Ruben said meekly. "Maybe so."

CHAPTER 14

1976

Midway through his second year in Durango, Edwin graduated from cot to a twin mattress and box spring he pushed against a wall. He slept so well he found he needed fewer hours of sleep. And so he found himself taking a late stroll in his robe to the cafeteria for a glass of milk after 10:30 one spring night. In the dimly lit hall beyond it where the clinic and women's dorm room were, Edwin heard a door creak open and a young man appeared outside the women's restroom. Matthew Paisley, a nineteen-year-old missionary from Kansas, walked briskly down the hall but stopped in his tracks when he saw Edwin in his path.

"Kinda late to be up, isn't it?" the bishop asked of the wide-eyed teenager. The boy, still in his work khakis and a half-tucked dress shirt, cupped his hands in front of his crotch.

"I . . . I had to use the restroom," the lanky blond said, fixing his eyes on the floor.

"So why go to the restroom at the far end of the

building?"

Paisley, his eyes darting about, hesitated a moment and stammered, "Cause our restroom was taken. Somebody stunk it up somethin' awful!"

Just then the restroom door creaked open a second time. "Randi," the hooker with orange hair, stepped softly out, wearing nothing but a towel. When she saw Edwin, she made for the dormitory room door.

"Hold it, Randi. I want a word," he said. "Go to bed, Matthew!"

When he reached her, Randi was glancing about the hall, mulling escape routes. She ran fingers through her mussed hair and guarded her loins, tugging at the flimsy towel that covered her.

"You and Matthew Paisley were in the bathroom together," Edwin said. "What happened in there?"

Randi swung her arms back and forth. "We were talkin', sir."

"What's that in your right hand," Edwin demanded. The hand was fisted. "Show me!" he said.

She opened her hand to reveal a $20 bill and flashed a guilty smile.

"Did you have sex?" he asked.

"No," she said. "I used my mouth."

Edwin's head swam. "And for how long now?"

"Didn't take long at all," she said.

"No, no, child. How long have missionaries been coming over here at night?"

"This was my first," she said. "But some of the other girls have done it a while."

"Just with Matthew?"

"Three or four come kinda regular."

"Christ!" said the bishop. "Go to bed Randi. And tell the other girls this is over!"

Edwin's legs felt heavy on the walk back to his office. He stripped off his slippers and robe and, switching off the light, nestled under a sheet and stared at a ceiling animated by moon rays from the far window. He took deep breaths to calm his racing heart. It pounded in his ears. "Focus man!" he said aloud.

A cloud began to shroud the moon, swaddling the bishop in moody darkness. It matched his dread as he replayed what had just happened; but it could not have happened, because it was unthinkable. Prostitution had come to his church; tender missionaries under his trusted care were nestling in the bosom of . . . of . . .

Bathed in sweat, he cast off his sheet despite the cool late air. It had come. A scandal of the highest order. If he singled out the offending missionaries, shipped them home and had the church nullify their missionary work, their parents back home would surely rampage at the stew of whores and boys simmering under one roof. They would demand his head and the Church would lop it off. The entire Durango mission, he feared, could be lopped from the Church tree as well.

"This is a smelly stink!" he cursed. The moon's reappearance through the window calmed him some, reminding him, as Mormon Elder Edwin Sr. once counseled, that "dark days are no match for the sunshine that follows."

He donned his robe and slippers and, taking a chair from his room, propped it against a hallway wall and spent the remainder of the night there. In the morning, he went about his duties as if nothing had happened.

When Teresa Cortez arrived that afternoon, he filled her in and announced, "We need a night watchman."

"Well I guess we shoulda seen that comin'," Red said by phone to Teresa later in the day. He was on one of his frequent trips to Juarez where he ran an adoption agency named Heavenly Connections. "Them boys smelled honey in that hive."

"I thought Mormons kept their zippers up?" said Teresa caustically.

"Most do," said Red. "But there're bad apples in every bushel."

"Well the bishop's figured out he has to keep this quiet. That's good," she said. "I'm gonna bring my daughter Juanita in at night to referee, starting tomorrow."

Edwin worked on the blueprints of the permanent mission. All regional temples followed a standardized Mormon style, but the bishops had flexibility to mold the interior layouts to their needs. It was taxing work. Juanita became Edwin's relief valve. Before the spring nights faded, the bishop sought her company more frequently. He'd quiz her on the book she was reading and field questions from her on Mormonism. Sometimes they talked for hours.

When Juanita turned twenty-one, the bishop had a birthday cake ready for her arrival. She came dressed in jeans and a white blouse tied at the waist to expose her midriff and stood with hands in pockets while the expectant mothers sang Happy Birthday. When Edwin gave her a hard cover copy of *Catcher in the Rye*, translated into Spanish, Juanita hugged the bishop warmly, and he blushed as his fingers felt the bare curves of her back.

Edwin preached abstinence that Sunday but only by

coincidence. "What greater gift can we give ourselves than purity of heart?" he had said. It was a message aimed mostly at the ward's tender missionaries. At the end of it, Edwin noticed Matthew Paisley's eyes had moistened. The next day, the guilted youngster asked to be transferred back home.

Edwin's mission tour was into its third year when the afternoon rains began to slacken. One night, as the bishop was preparing for bed a knock came and his door swung open. Juanita entered briskly, intent on foraging for a new book, but stopped and placed her hand to her lips in surprise. Edwin was shirtless and his khaki shorts were half unzipped, exposing his briefs. Their eyes met and she blushed but quickly composed herself, marching resolutely to the bookcase, where she fumbled among the volumes. Finding one, she glanced his way a last time and wished him a good night. Making no move to cover himself, he shrugged and eased into his chair.

By midnight, the church was dark and quiet. Juanita was absorbed in her book when she heard a key unlock the church's main door. Teresa Cortez entered and, with a quick nod to her daughter, disappeared into the clinic. In minutes, Angel, bulging with child, appeared in the hallway with Teresa, who stopped in front of Juanita.

"I'll be gone two to three days," she said. "It's Angel's time and we're off to Juarez. There's a couple waiting for the baby in El Paso."

Juanita nodded her understanding.

"This is the time we talked about," the midwife said. "After Angel there's Delores, then Brandi."

"I know," Juanita said.

"He's asleep?" she said, referring to the bishop.

"I caught him half undressed tonight when I went looking for a book," she said. "My guess is he's thinking of me."

"Are you nervous?"

"No, mother. I'll handle things here. Don't worry." The following night hosted a new moon, a mere sliver, which left the school's halls darker than usual. After settling in and making sure everyone was bedded down, Juanita took a sponge bath in the women's restroom and walked into the hall clad in only a towel.

Edwin, coming out of the cafeteria, turned to her and nearly choked on a swig of milk. The towel barely covered Juanita's hips and her pretty legs were long and languid. He drank her in with gawking eyes. Feigning embarrassment, she giggled at his milk moustache then turned her back to him and walked slowly back to the restroom, exposing two inches of her milky bottom.

Edwin felt a stiffness in his loins. For a moment he thought of following her, then chastised himself. Practice what you preach, he said to himself, and padded down the hall to his room and read until eleven.

When finally he turned off his light, he marveled at how the darkness cloaked the room. He was almost asleep when he heard the door click open. He could not see her but sensed her presence. He heard something fall to the floor; a towel perhaps. He felt the sheets being lifted, he held his breath, and she was beside him.

CHAPTER 15

2002 DAY FOUR

On a Sunday, Ruben returned to Rosa's house to say goodbye.

Rosa was still in her new dress. Ruben, in blue jeans and a T-shirt, pressed a wad of pesos into her hand.

"I'll be back in a few months with my daughter," he told her.

She fixed on his eyes and they were silent. Shifting his weight from one foot to the other, Ruben struggled for words. "I'll write every week," he said finally.

"I can't read. Emilia will read your letters to me," she said. "I will go to the post office each week to see what you have sent." She smiled at Ruben and took his hand in hers.

"Thank you for coming," Rosa said gently. "I love you."

They embraced a final time before Ruben drove to see Lomas. Everyone was home. After visiting a few minutes inside, Lomas walked Ruben to the car.

"You'll be a thousand miles from here by tonight?" Lomas asked, struggling to come to terms with travel in a world far more modern than his own. "That's amazing to me. What does it feel like in a jet plane?"

Ruben laughed. "It's a little scary the first time," he said, smiling. "They go really fast and you're so high up you can see everything, sometimes for hundreds of miles."

"I've never been out of Durango," Lomas admitted. "Someday I want to go with my family to the coast. I'd like to catch a sailfish. I've seen pictures of them as big as a man."

"I saw some like that in Zihuatanejo a few days ago," Ruben said. "The people in the market said fishing is good there this time of year."

"Someday," Lomas said casually. "In the meantime, I hope you will speak well of us to your family."

"You are my family now, as well," Ruben said. "That reminds me. You spent a long time looking at the photo of my wife and daughter over dinner. Was there something that caught your attention?"

Lomas looked surprised. "I'm sorry, Ruben. I didn't mean to stare. It's nothing."

"No, it's okay. I was just curious," Ruben said.

Lomas shifted his gaze to a family crossing the street on their way to church. They were spiffed up for the occasion, with the husband in dress boots and his three children in school clothes.

"I see a resemblance between your wife and Rosa," Lomas said timidly. "I know that sounds weird . . . and I guess it is weird . . . but it's there. Emelia saw it, too. Course, I do this all the time. It's been over twenty years since Maria went missing but I still find myself searching for her in other people's faces. This is not the first time. I should not have mentioned it."

"Don't apologize," said Ruben. "Was there something

in particular?"

"I think it was your wife's big smile. When I was much younger, Mama used to smile like that," Lomas said.

"I would love to see that in Rosa myself," said Ruben. He shook Lomas' hand and headed for the airport.

Awaiting his flight, Ruben idly pulled out the photos he'd developed of Rosa and compared her to Rebecca from the family photo in his wallet. His first inclination was to dismiss Lomas' perceptions entirely; placing Rosa's leathery face next to his wife's was like posing prune to plum. But he did notice something; though Rosa was only grinning so as not to reveal her teeth, the pattern of her upturned lips formed a crease of skin on either side that Rebecca mimicked with her beaming smile. It highlighted the full lips of both women and Ruben noted it with interest. A small thing, yes, but something.

He put away the photos and closed his eyes, trying to shut out the ambient noise of the small but busy airport. He yearned to be home, with his wife and daughter. The PA system crackling with arrival and departure announcements brought his thoughts back to Durango. Looking at his watch, he grimaced. He was an hour shy of departure on a flight to Mexico City, then Utah.

An expectant mother in maternity jeans and a pleated blouse eased into a seat across from Ruben and dug in her carry-on bag for something to eat. She looked to be in her early twenties, he thought, and he found himself studying her face. When she noticed and returned a glassy stare, Ruben squinted awkwardly and looked away. He caught himself doing the same thing as another young Mexican woman walked in his direction shepherding two young children. She briefly smiled at him as she passed.

Ruben chastised himself. He was ogling women in a public airport as if they were models on a runway, seeking traces of a sister he never knew. It bothered him to think such a vexing habit had haunted Lomas for much of his life. Ruben slumped in his chair and stared at his sandaled feet. After debating with himself for fifteen minutes, idly twisting his wedding ring in his fingers, he rose, headed to the airline counter and cancelled his flight home.

CHAPTER 16

Ruben phoned his wife that he was delaying his return to Utah an extra day, which gave him the rest of Sunday to do as he pleased. He drove to downtown Durango, parked his rental, and walked to the open courtyard of the town square, tree-lined and ringed with street vendors, where he toured the landmark Cathedral of Durango towering above the inner city.

Among the vendors he noticed a dizzying array of amber and clear molded plastic trinkets encasing scorpions like the one he'd seen in Rosa's casucha. They were everywhere; on neck chains, as bookends, glued to the butts of hunting knives, toy swords, walking canes and on the handles of pistols. The lore of the scorpion in Durango was as old as the city itself. The most feared and revered of them was the white scorpion, the vendors cautioned; capable of delivering enough venom to make it a killer of children, women, and all but the strongest men. Beware the smaller ones, they said, because an immature scorpion delivers all its venom in one sting while the older ones use just enough to immobilize their prey, always keeping some in reserve.

How so many scorpions could be found in a place such as Durango was a mystery to Ruben. There were more than enough to satisfy all the tourists who hungered for things that came wrapped in a good story.

Hunger drove Ruben east, to the city's largest outdoor market and a stuffed pepper that set his mouth on fire and took two Cokes to put out.

As evening descended on the city, with big-sky clouds sponging up the reds and oranges of a sinking sun, Ruben sauntered in and out of pastel-splashed shops fronting the paved, wide streets of a modern-day Durango that seemed generations removed from Rosa Segovia's barren barrio. Streetlights flickered on, buses loaded and unloaded locals in sharp-creased slacks and designer jeans and outdoor restaurants teemed with after-workers. They were like so many stick people to Ruben, interchangeable with the stick people of any other big city: Cardboard cutouts you could place anywhere and they would look the same.

Waiting for sleep to overtake him that night, Ruben's thoughts drifted homeward, to Megan's excitement over her first bicycle and then to the bicycle with a red bow on the handlebars leaning on its kickstand Christmas morning when he was six. It was black and shiny with knobby tires and he recalled learning to ride it in twenty minutes to the delight of his winded father. By that afternoon, he was exploring streets with his parents beyond his own. The streets were shiny, too, like discovered diamonds to a child's eye: inviting, mysterious, new.

The imagery reminded Ruben of how he was raised, with windows to the outside world opening to him gradually, one pane at a time. His parents monitored the doses of reality he ingested; a spoonful here and there; mindful there are many ways the world can rub the luster from the innocence of youth.

They censored his internet access and the movies he watched and took care to limit his friends to other Mormons. Worldly wonders creeped in anyway; Ruben recalling the first nudie foldout he saw with a flashlight beneath a bedroll at a Boy Scout campout and the embarrassing wet dreams that followed. His first kiss produced something similar; awkward fumbling happened on occasion but like most teenagers Ruben mostly fumbled with himself. When he and Rebecca consummated their marriage, both were virgins. Though clumsy as lovers, they were typical of Mormon youth, practicing abstinence until the honeymoon.

Ruben blinked the wedding night briefly into focus, lying naked with Rebecca in the posh honeymoon suite of the airport Marriott in Provo, feeling his body energized, alive. Blinking again, he was back in his cheap Durango motel room with bare walls and the hum of the window AC unit lulling him, finally, toward sleep.

In the morning, Ruben rose early and drove to the Durango central police station with only a shred of hope he'd find what he was after. He knew which year he sought, as well as the season but little else.

A uniformed records clerk, ensconced behind an old gray desk with nothing on it but the officer's feet, sized up Ruben as cheap fluorescent lightbulbs strobed above him in the bowels of the station house. "What can I do for you senor?" he asked, poking his head from behind a flea market insert he'd scavenged from the daily newspaper.

"Good morning," Ruben said briskly. "I'm looking for

a police report on a kidnapping twenty-three years ago."

"What on earth for?" the man asked.

"It's my sister who was kidnapped," Ruben said. "She's still missing. I'm hoping the report will help me find her."

"These are official police records," the clerk said sternly. "I don't let just anybody see them."

"If you'll help me," Ruben began, reaching for his wallet. "I'll give you one hundred dollars American."

The clerk's eyed widened. Ruben's offer was almost a month's pay. He sat up, glanced about the empty records room, and then put out his hand.

"What date?" he asked.

"The year was 1976, in the Spring."

The clerk pocketed the five twenty-dollar bills and said, "Have a seat. This may take a while."

After fifteen minutes passed, Ruben feared he'd been had. "Shouldn't have given him the money up front," Ruben mumbled, scolding himself. He rose and tried to peer down row after row of metal shelves bulging with labeled files behind the clerk's desk. At the end of the last one, Ruben spied the clerk ambling toward him pushing a loaded down grocery cart.

The files were stored by year and crime. There were two 1976 categories in the cart, kidnapping and missing persons. "Your sister's case will probably be in the missing persons folders unless someone actually witnessed the crime," the clerk said. Eight missing person folders, each containing at least fifty individual reports were stacked with two folders of kidnapping cases.

Ruben was instantly emersed in stories of tragedy condensed to the just-the-facts staccato of beat cops and detectives. Pedro went to drink with friends and never returned home. Alexandra, thought by her parents to have a boyfriend in Torreon, was believed to have gone to him but she hadn't packed a bag. Missing persons who weren't missed until long after they disappeared; coworkers who stopped showing up for work, drug abusers who'd slunk away. For hours Ruben scanned them, through folder after folder, until he reached folder four. The reports were faded and the paper brittle, and he used just two fingers to lift each one to the light.

The clerk was losing patience. His shift, up at three, would soon be done. He looked to Ruben, who had stopped reading and was staring blankly at the wall.

"Senor, have you found what you seek?" he asked.

Ruben nodded and bowed his head before asking for copies of the two-page document concerning Maria Segovia.

He staggered into the daylight with his shoulders drooped, trudging deliberately to his car, ignoring the stick people bustling beside him. One of them accidentally bumped against him and Ruben lurched at him, pushing him rudely away. At the car door, he wiped his runny nose with his shirt sleeve and climbed slowly in. He reread the report and shook his head in disbelief. On page two, under a description of Maria, it noted she was wearing a pale blue dress when kidnapped and she had "a crescent moon shaped birthmark on her left hip".

CHAPTER 17

Angeline Vega pruned roses in the backyard of her Provo home as dusk caressed her cheeks with a breath of cool air, prompting an involuntary shudder. She looked up, scanning the clear autumn skies for further proof of the day's creep toward dusk but seeing only the streak of a jet's trail far above spreading thinly like ice over water, she resumed to her task, clipping the last of six white roses destined for a vase on the dining room table.

Seconds later, her husband, Joe, stepped onto the porch.

She eyed him curiously. "Who called?" she asked, having heard the phone ring minutes earlier.

"Ruben," said Joe, whose thin mustache dangled from the sides of a frown. "He called to ask if Rebecca was adopted."

Angeline's mouth dropped open. "What?" she stammered, accidentally pinching a finger between the shear's handles. "Ow!" She winced and shook her hand to shoo the pain. "But how could he have known? Becky doesn't even know!"

Joe shrugged. "He said he was calling from Mexico and

had come across something that disturbed him, something about a birthmark like Becky's on a baby who was kidnapped twenty something years ago. He said the baby was his sister."

Angeline Vega, swatting a loose hair strand that drooped beside her right eye, stared blankly at her husband. "What?" she stammered. "Kidnapped?"

"Yeah," he said. "I told him our Becky was born in Chihuahua to an unwed teen who gave her up for adoption when she was three months old. We have the papers. The mother gave her consent.

"Then he wants to know who handled the adoption, who put the baby in our hands and if Edwin was involved. It became an interrogation. You know how he gets sometimes. He was browbeating me. Then he hung up. No goodbye. Just 'Click,' Gone." he added. "What does it mean?"

"It means trouble," she said, rising quickly to brush the dirt off her jeans. "We'd better call Becky right now before Ruben does."

"Becky . . . Becky . . . Becky!"

Sitting on the edge of her bed, Rebecca reached down and snared the phone from the floor. It had slipped through her fingers and fallen face down, muffling the voices on the other end. She drew a breath.

"This is life altering!" Rebecca whimpered with the phone back to her ear. "And you didn't plan to tell me? Ever?"

Joe Vega spoke up. "We thought it best not to tell you

when you were young. As you got older, we went back and forth on it. We have friends with adopted kids and some of them haven't told their children either."

"Like who?" Rebecca blurted out. "Oh, I don't care . . . everything I've ever known about myself is a lie."

"We didn't tell you because we wanted you to have a normal childhood, at school, with your friends," Angeline said. "If you knew you were adopted, you might have been self-conscious about it, less self-assured. We wanted you to grow up as normal as the other kids."

"Well, I'm no kid now," Rebecca said indignantly. "Who's my mother?"

"Someone in Chihuahua," said Joe. "We've got the papers. They told us she was an unwed teen."

"So, some floozy was my real mom?" She let herself fall backward onto the bed and closed her eyes, fighting off the urge to cry.

"It was a young girl who got pregnant and who was too young to be a good mother," said Angeline. "She tried to raise you but ended up putting you up for adoption. That's all we know."

"How did Ruben know about it?"

"He didn't say," said her father. "We didn't talk long."

Rebecca began to whine. "Something's wrong with him, I know it," she intoned. "He hasn't phoned all day. I don't even know when he's coming home. How did he sound?"

"Angry," said Joe.

--

Across town, the phone rang at the Youngblood home.

"This is an international operator for AT&T. Is this Edwin Youngblood?"

"Yes."

"I have a collect call for you from Ruben Youngblood. Will you accept the charges?

"Of course."

"Connecting."

"Son?"

"Did you know anything about a string of baby kidnappings in Durango while you were there?" Ruben asked. He was standing at a phone booth inside a farmacia.

"Why?"

"I found my mother. And I have an older brother. I also have a younger sister who was kidnapped as a baby."

"Oh, no!" Edwin said.

"The police report from back then said there had been a number of baby kidnappings. Did you know anything about that?" Ruben asked.

"I saw something in the local paper about that, I'm pretty sure. Didn't think much about it," said Edwin.

"I pulled up one of those stories on the newspaper's archive. They quoted a woman whose son was kidnapped. It took me all day, but I found her and talked to her. Still in the same place she always was, just like Rosa," said Ruben. "Turns out there was a common thread between my sister's disappearance and that woman's son."

"Oh?"

"They both had the same midwife, Teresa Cortez."

Edwin was silent.

"You think it's possible any members of your little adoption network were mixed up in those kidnappings?" Ruben asked, his tone now accusatory.

"No!" Edwin blurted. "She was a midwife to lots of people back then. That doesn't make her a kidnapper. Now stop all this and get yourself back home."

"Gotta go visit your old buddy Red in El Paso first. Then maybe we'll know if you're right."

Edwin heard a click followed by the low tone of an ended call.

Ruben stood in the pharmacy and wiped the sweat from his forehead. His face felt flushed, on fire. He scanned the faces around him; locals all, shopping and herding children. Don't they know to keep their distance, he wondered. His fists were clenching involuntarily and when a young boy strode up, Ruben glared at him and quickly walked outside, drove to the central market, and asked around for four things: duct tape, live scorpions, a blue steel handgun, and bullets.

CHAPTER 18

2002 – DAY SIX

By the look of him, Red in 2002 was lumpy scrap metal, as road-weary as the spike-finned Ford Fairlane he relegated to the junk pile in late 1976 in favor of the first of his three Cadillacs. His elbows were knobby and calloused, his legs varicosed. He was swollen with ballast, from his pregnant belly to his baggy eyes, double chin, and thick ankles. The burnt orange hair on his neck, arms, and legs, gave him the hue of rust.

He owed the cane he used to diabetes, which robbed him of decent circulation in his right leg. He limped like a flat-tired jalopy and it hurt to walk when the leg acted up which was often.

As Red wheeled his Caddy into the driveway of his suburban home a quarter mile north of the Rio Grande, Ruben was watching from his rental car half a block away. He'd tracked him easily: the city directory at the downtown library nestled him in the residential pages between Stanley Pierce and Steven W Pierce.

His place was tract-home nondescript, bricked in front

with siding elsewhere; ranch-style and small.

"Gawd damn it all!" Red shouted, stubbing his bad foot on the car door with grocery bags on each arm. He talked to himself all the way to the front door and Ruben craned his neck to hear. He gleaned the comment "broke down mule," when Red sat down a grocery bag to fish for his keys.

Ruben watched the house for half the morning to make sure Red was alone. When he appeared again in an undershirt and baggy shorts, returning to the car for his cane, Ruben leaped from his rental and, sprinting, came up behind as Red re-crossed the door threshold. Ruben stuck a pistol against his back, wrestled his cane away and walked him into the den, kicking the front door shut. He had one arm on Red's shoulder, guiding the big man toward a chair in the den, where he pushed him down and moved like a spider encircling prey, using duct tape to trap him.

"Who're you?" Red clamored, trying to shake off his shock. Ruben had his torso and arms wrapped in seconds, moving in wide circles around the chair. "What's this about?"

"I'm from your past, Red," Ruben said, reaching low to wrap Red's left ankle to the chair leg. But when he moved to the other Red caught him in the chin with his foot, which threw Ruben backward to the floor. Ruben rose and delivered a solid right hook to Red's jaw, which quieted the Tennessean. He taped Red's second leg to the chair, slipped off his backpack and peered between the front window shades to take the neighborhood's pulse.

"Now let me introduce myself," he said, turning from the window. "I'm Ruben Youngblood, the son of Bishop

Edwin Youngblood. You remember him, don't you?"

Red's bottom lip was oozing blood onto his T-shirt. He used his tongue to gauge the swelling. "Edwin Youngblood's a friend o' mine," he said angrily. "Why you got cause to hurt me?"

"Because you and this adoption ring may have ruined my life, Red. Tell me, did my father know you were kidnapping babies?"

Red's angry eyes riveted on Ruben. "You're a nut ball, ain'tcha?" he growled. "Nobody kidnapped no babies!"

"Oh, but you did, and I think I can prove it. If I decide not to kill you."

Red scowled. "Them adoptions were legit. Now let me go afore I get mad!"

"Can't do that, Red," Ruben said. He headed for the kitchen, rifling through counter drawers until he found a clean dish towel. By the time he returned, Red was howling.

"Help!" he bellowed toward the front windows; his voice thunderous. "Help!" he screamed again just as Ruben shoved half the towel in Red's mouth.

"That's better." He walked to the window, surveying the street through the half-closed blinds. He saw no movement, not even a passing car.

"Now I need to look at your old adoption files. I drove by your old agency office and saw you're selling bail bonds now. So I'm thinking you've probably got the files right here. In the garage maybe?"

Ruben ambled through the kitchen, opened the door beside the pantry and flipped on the garage light. He scanned the cluttered contents. On one side a work bench sat beside a table saw next to a lathe. Large toolboxes, with open drawers bulging with wrenches and screwdrivers were against a nearby wall. On the other side lawn equipment hung from wall racks. A four-shelf storage unit contained dusty boxes of all shapes and sizes on the top three shelves. But the lower shelf was empty. When he examined it, he could see a dust trail where something had been dragged into the center of the garage.

Ruben frowned and went back in the house.

"He tipped you off, didn't he?" Ruben said angrily to Red. "Edwin told you I was coming. You were easy enough to find. That's what happened, isn't it?"

Red stared defiantly.

"He must be as worried about what's in those records as you are, Red, and I think I know why."

Turning his back to Red, Ruben crossed the den and disappeared down the hall, reappearing minutes later with a three-foot-square cardboard box he rummaged from a bedroom closet. He sat it down beside Red's feet, walked behind him and tilted the chair backwards, raising the front legs of it. He slid the box under Red's feet and then lowered the chair down so his feet and the chair legs were inside it. He secured the box in place.

Standing over Red, Ruben reached into his backpack and retrieved a sandwich bag with six scorpions inside. He waved the bag inches from Red's face.

Red's eyes bulged. He shook his head furiously from side to side. "Nmhmmmm!" he mouthed.

"Now I'm gonna need you to tell me where you stashed those files. And if you don't, these beauties are going in that box at your feet." Ruben removed the towel from Red's mouth.

The anger in Red's eyes was gone, replaced by wide-eyed fright. He tried shaking himself loose from his restraints but succeeded in knocking over the chair instead. He landed hard on his right side, bumping his head on the carpet, and shrieked in pain.

Ruben calmly shook his head. "That probably won't be a good idea once I put these scorpions in the box, Red. That'll agitate them some, don't you think?"

Red, dizzy from the fall, stopped pulling against the tape and went limp as Ruben tried to right the chair. But it was like lifting 300 pounds of dead weight and Ruben couldn't do it. After mulling options, he finally wedged one arm under the right side of the chair and the other on the chair back and pushed upward, using his legs to do the lifting until the chair righted itself.

"Now, the files?" said Ruben.

Red moaned his surrender. "Top drawer of the desk in the bedroom," he said.

Inside it Ruben found paperwork from a storage unit Red had rented earlier that morning, along with a key to the lock and entry instructions. Stuffing the towel back in Red's mouth, Ruben gingerly placed the sealed sandwich bag inside the box by Red's feet.

"Be right back."

He returned within an hour with two files in his hand. He'd loaded the other files in his trunk. He sat at the breakfast table off the kitchen where the light was good and opened the file marked Baby Vega. The birth certificate was in the name of Verona Castillo, daughter of a nineteen-year-old mother from Cuidad Chihuahua, 225 miles south of Juarez. The birth date was Oct. 4, 1979, Rebecca's given birthday. Maria's birthday, according to the police kidnapping report, was Oct. 22, 1979, a two-week difference. Ruben pondered that and concluded the difference was meaningless since using the same birthday would give the kidnappers away. He examined the two-page relinquishment of parental rights with a crude signature - not in cursive but in single letters - scrawled at the bottom. Other adoption papers, including an application from Joe and Angeline Vega and a judge's consent, were there. No photos were included.

The last page contained what looked to be a doctor's notes, with height, weight, hair color and, finally, a note of caution: "Milk allergy. Use soy-based formula." There was no mention of any birth marks.

The file of Baby Youngblood had less heft to it. The birth certificate matched the one that Edwin had given to Ruben, and the parental rights form appeared to contain the signature of Rosa Ramon Segovia.

Birth certificates for both babies were signed by Teresa Cortez, midwife.

"I'm gonna need to use your phone," Ruben advised Red. He placed a collect call to the Vega residence. Angeline answered.

"Hi, Angeline, it's Ruben. When you picked up Becky in El Paso, did she have a milk allergy?" he asked.

"What is this about, Ruben?" she demanded.

"I don't have time to talk about it now. Just tell me please."

She was silent for a moment, then responded: "Yes, we were told to give her a soy formula. She outgrew the allergy within a year. Now ..."

She heard a click and the line went silent.

When Ruben returned to the living room, Red noticed his shoulders were slumped and his gait slower. Red, swallowing hard as Ruben withdrew the sandwich bag from the box, stared intently at the scorpions huddled together.

"Now before I release these, I'll tell what you've done," Ruben said, speaking slowly. He leaned down in front of Red, so he met his eyes. "I came to Mexico to track down my mother. When I found her, I learned I had a half-sister who'd been kidnapped after I was born. She was later adopted, through your agency."

Red stared blankly.

"The people who adopted her are Mormons who knew my father. And what did they do? They introduced her to me. And what did I do? I married her!

"You're a Mormon or you pretend to be. So surely you understand its teachings about family and the afterlife. Rebecca and I were each sealed in the temple by our adoptive parents. But if we're brother and sister, the seals are broken. There will be no afterlife."

Ruben, his eyes suddenly heavy, gazed absently toward the window.

"She's all I ever wanted, you know?" he said quietly. "Becky's her name. We have a daughter. She's like air to me. Without her I won't have a reason to breathe."

Ruben stared for a long time at Red and the contraption he'd built for him. Then he asked: "You have a picture of your wives in the bedroom. What happened to them?"

He removed the towel from his mouth. Red greedily sucked in air.

"Gone. Long gone," he said finally. "They took the two boys, one each. Didn't need me around much after they came along. Them gals were lovers, you know?

"Yep. Moved back to Humboldt twelve years ago now. Bought a place in the country." Red shrugged. "I get a letter now and then. Sometimes they send along photos of the boys. They're bigguns, like their dad."

"Well that's good and bad, I guess," Ruben intoned. "Now how do you suppose my kidnapped sister ended up at your adoption agency, Red?"

Red shook his head. "What kind of scorpions are those?"

"The bad kind, Red. White scorpions from Durango. I hear they pack one hell of a wallop. Now about my sister . . ."

"Your dad ever mention the name Teresa Cortez?" Red asked. "She's a midwife."

"She ran the clinic, I know," Ruben said. "She also signed most of the birth certificates in those adoption files."

"She dealt with all the preggies, some from the clinic and those she met through her work in the barrios. Anyway, it got to where the demand for babies was bigger than our inventory and I remember we talked about it on the phone one time. And she asked me 'What about older babies. Is there a market for them?'

"And I says 'I reckon, if you find women willin' to give 'em up. They usually get attached if they're older, don't they?'

"She says 'Let me worry about that.'

"Seems like we did have some babies brought in that were, I dunno, three or more months old. Teresa had parental release forms on all of 'em so I didn't think much about it. We probably had ten or more like that.

"Now that's all I know and that's the gall durn truth," he said. "Now let me go."

"Tell me where to find Cortez and this guy Marmoles," Ruben demanded.

Red obliged and gave Ruben directions. Then he watched helplessly as Ruben began duct taping the top of the box until there was a small slit left open. He opened the baggy and slipped it inside. He gave it a shake and in rapid motion retrieved the bag and stuffed it into his backpack. He put the towel back in Red's mouth and taped it in place.

"You're in luck," Ruben deadpanned. "Your odds just got better. I just put two in there. Now they're pretty angry right now so I suggest you stay very still until they calm down."

Red barely heard. He was riveted on the box, which Ruben sealed with one more piece of tape. He imagined the hideous freaks of nature hovering by his foot, pincers out, preparing to stab him with their stingers. Red was careful not to twitch his toes. Sweat beaded on his forehead and along his arms.

Ruben watched a moment and then gathered his belongings and walked out the front door.

Red sat catlike, concentrating for all he was worth.

CHAPTER 19

Rebecca faced Edwin in his study. Both were in leather chairs with thick armrests. Rebecca tried to disappear in hers. She scrunched her legs against her chest and wrapped her arms around them.

Edwin, wearing a summer robe over a T-shirt and khakis, sipped greedily at his coffee. He had slept later than usual after another fitful night. Looking at him, Rebecca felt it necessary to apologize for her early arrival, though it was after eight.

"You're not early," he soothed. "I'm just out of sync."

In another room, Rebecca could hear Megan and Gabby laughing.

"So . . . you found out yesterday you were adopted from Mexico," said Edwin, squinting at Rebecca through puffy eyes. "Big shock, I'm sure."

"Pretty big," she said, frowning. She cast her eyes toward the window behind Edwin, where a soft rain tapped at the panes. "You knew all along, of course."

"Yes. I knew," he said. "We've been friends with your parents a long, long time. But we never told Ruben. He figured that out on his own."

"But how could he have?" she asked nervously. "He was supposed to be looking for his sister."

"I don't know, sweetheart," said Edwin. "We're going to have to get that answer from him."

Rebecca was silent, distracted by the shadows the raindrops cast on the windows before snaking to the sill. "Tell me how you found Ruben," she said.

"Oh?" he said. "Well, I'm afraid, my dear, that is a subject that will require more coffee."

He rose slowly, using his arms to push himself up, and padded to the kitchen, where Megan was spooning for raisins in her cereal while Gabby read from a Dr. Seuss book. As he returned to his seat, he patted Rebecca on the head.

"Megan is adorable, Becky," he said smiling. "I'm so glad you two were able to have a child. It's a real gift, you know?"

"We know, Dad. And thanks," she said, smiling. She relaxed her grip on her legs and let them settle to the floor as Edwin grasped his coffee cup with both hands, blowing softly on the mixture before gulping some down.

"I'm going to tell you what I told Ruben a year or so ago," Edwin said. "We did some good things in Durango, some things I'm very proud of. But there were mistakes made. I trusted people who took advantage."

He paused and looked at Rebecca, who had begun rubbing her temples. "Mistakes?" As she said it, she began to curl back up into a semi-fetal position in the chair.

"Nothing to be scared of," he said. "What I did wasn't illegal, but it was borderline. I accepted that some corners had to be cut so I could unite unwanted babies with couples in the U.S.; people like you and your parents,

Becky. But in the process, I lined some people's pockets and I was too trusting, too preoccupied with other things to see it."

Megan's laughter crept suddenly into the room. She had run into the hall and was directly outside the study, shrieking with excitement as Gabby chased her through the house. Edwin's lips curled into a smile.

"I'm rambling," he said.

"No, not at all. You'll just have to compete with Megan for the floor," Rebecca said.

"Anytime," he said. "Anyway, there was this expatriate who joined the ward in Durango named Sterling Pierce and he and I hit it off pretty well, though I'm not sure why. I mean, we weren't much alike. He was a schemer but he was always willing to help out in the beginning; he worked part time for a lawyer down there.

"One day this mother left her newborn at the church and ran off so Red . . . that's Sterling's nickname . . . talked to his lawyer friend, Eduard Marmoles, about what to do. Next day, Red says he's worked everything out and was going to turn the baby over to an adoption agency in Juarez.

"That's how it started. After a while, other women came to us, some with babies and some still pregnant. We set up a group home for the pregnant ones, which included a goodly number of prostitutes, and I hired this midwife named Teresa Cortez to run it and deliver the babies. The locals called it the incubator. Word got out in Durango that women could get their babies adopted in the U.S. through there."

"Why would they want that?" Rebecca wondered.

"Desperation; a longing to give their children a better

life," he said. "You can't imagine how some of those people lived. They didn't have food or clothes or running water or toilets. Many times their husbands went to the States to work and never came back. I'm convinced that those mothers who gave their children away loved them as much as you love Megan; they did it to give them a life outside the barrio."

Rebecca rocked back and forth before nodding her understanding.

"I came to believe we shouldn't turn those mothers away," he continued. "And I leaned pretty heavily on Red to take care of a lot of the details. That was a mistake. Behind my back, he and his lawyer friend set up their own adoption agency in El Paso, with a way station in Juarez and used the midwife to take the mothers across the border when they were ready to deliver. That way the babies were born U.S. citizens. The ones left at our doorstep or who gave birth prematurely were brought into the U.S. by coyotes posing as their mothers. Those babies had forged birth certificates."

Edwin paused and lowered his head.

"Isn't that against the law?" Rebecca stammered.

"Course it is, sweetie," said Edwin.

"Then why didn't you stop it?" said Rebecca. She stared at her father-in-law, incredulous.

"Because I didn't know about it," he said. "Red and Cortez led me to believe our only role was to get the babies to the adoption agency and the agency took it from there. It wasn't until things started to unravel after I'd left Durango that I learned we were in deeper than that.

"My first clue was when I got a call from a guy in Utah who wanted to know if I was personally sanctioning all of

Red's adoptions and if so, he wanted his money back. This guy tells me he'd paid a $5,000 deposit on a baby and hadn't heard back from Red. He sent me a copy of the brochure the adoption agency sent with all these inflated expenses; like $1,000 for hospital bills, a $1,500 finder's fee, translation fees, court costs, room and board for the mothers-to-be and even money to pay babysitters, all totaling $15,000.

"Of course, there were no hospital bills, no finders to pay and the room and board was free, courtesy of our mission. Red, Marmoles, and Cortez got rich!"

As she listened, Rebecca stared blankly at the window behind Edwin. The rain had stopped and the window was illuminated in the bright morning sun. She couldn't seem to take her eyes away, in part because she didn't want to meet Edwin's eyes.

"Did you report what you learned to the police in Durango?" she asked.

"How could I? I was more or less an accomplice," he said. "Anyway, I couldn't drag the church into a scandal like that."

"But you're a good man, an honest man," she said, her eyes beseeching his. "How could things have gone so wrong?"

"I was focused on so many things back then, Becky," he said. "I put my trust in other's hands."

Rebecca's ears pounded in the unfolding silence. Edwin stared at his coffee cup and idly stirred the hot brew with his finger.

"You didn't tell me how you found Ruben," Rebecca said finally.

"Gabby was there helping me settle affairs at the end

of my mission and Cortez showed up with this beautiful baby one day and gave him to Gabby while I was out. It was love at first sight. I couldn't say no.

"I learned from other bishops in Utah that Red did about a dozen more adoptions for Mormon couples before things kind of dried up.

"I remember our return to Provo like it was yesterday," he said, diverting his eyes to a far wall as though some movie reel had clicked on there. "At the airport, dozens of parents held their adopted babies high in the air, showing them off. And Gabby and I held up ours, too. It was my mission that brought them there. It was magical.

"There was a big soiree at the ward hall with couples from all over the country there. They took a placard I'd made in Durango that said *A life without purpose is a lamp never lit* and attached it to the pulpit above a table with a list of the babies. They gave me a nickname, 'the Lamp Lighter.'

He returned his glance to Rebecca and she could see the tears in his eyes. "Imagine that," he said.

CHAPTER 20

Crossing the border back into Mexico with four boxes of adoption records in his trunk, Ruben breathed a sigh of relief. At a Juarez gas station, he filled the tank. In the restroom, he cringed at his reflection. His unshaven face sagged, his eyelids were swollen and sleep deprived, his forehead worry-creased. He decided to re-don his Panama hat, which he'd left in his travel bag in the car. By three he was on the road again, driving due south into the endless desert of the State of Chihuahua, where yuccas grow to the size of men; unbowed against the night wind, thriving in the heat. Creatures great and small; tarantulas, beaded lizards, even coyotes use their scant shade as way stations for daily survival.

He had time to think of his father's betrayal, which ached like a wound. But more than anything, his thoughts were on Rebecca. She would be worried sick and Megan would be clinging to her, concerned she might be the cause of her mother's pain. In silence he wept, wiped his eyes, and then pulled the brim of his hat low on his forehead, like an outlaw's camouflage.

If the nightmare is true, he decided, he could never see

them again.

In Ciudad, Chihuahua, a bustling place anchored by industrial parks and more than a dozen maquiladoras, the desert faded to lush parks and tree-lined streets. Ruben could find no barrios there; even the slums had streetlights, paving and curbs, stop signs and corner shops. But what it didn't have was 331 Calle Cielo Azul, the address listed for Rebecca's biological mother. It didn't exist on any maps. He drove to city hall and in the street department's files learned a Calle Cielo and Calle Azul existed but no combination of the two. He drove to both streets. It was late afternoon when he reached 331 Calle Azul, a simple hacienda of concrete block on a treeless street of homes with tall mortar fences backing up to more of the same, block after concrete block. When Ruben knocked, he could hear children racing to the door. A slender teenaged boy opened it. Behind him were two toddlers, a boy and a girl. No, the older boy said, no one named Castillo lived there. They were the Garcia family. The mother appeared at the door soon afterward, casting a wary glance at Ruben. She was dressed in an apron sprinkled with white flour.

"Do I know you?" she asked in Spanish.

"No," he said, smiling from beneath his hat. He quickly removed it and ran his fingers through his thick hair. "My wife, from America, was adopted and her birth certificate says her mother lived here. Her name was Verona Castillo. She would have lived here twenty-three years ago."

"We have lived here, always," said the woman. "My husband was born here."

"Then I have the wrong house," Ruben said. "I'm sorry. Your children are very polite."

"They would open the door to the devil," she said ruefully. "Good luck to you."

Calle Cielo was to the south, near a tire plant that made the air taste of burnt fabric and tar for miles. Ruben's nostrils burned as he walked to house number 331. No one answered there. He canvassed the neighborhood. No one knew of a Castillo family ever living there.

Back in his car, Ruben confronted the realization that Rebecca hadn't come from Chihuahua. He was on a snipe hunt; misled to chase a fictitious person down a non-existent street. He was Alice at the rabbit hole; with no rabbit to follow down.

Ruben booked a room on Chihuahua's outskirts and placed a call to the El Paso Police Department. He alerted a dispatcher there was a disturbance at the home of Sterling Pierce. Then he hung up. Three hours later, after a trip to the local Fedex office, Ruben strode into a tequila bar, pulled up a stool and plunked down $250 pesos.

Below the brim of his Panama hat, he peered through the long mirror behind the bar at a group of men huddled on their feet, drinking mugs of beer and talking loudly. There were two other men at the far end of the bar, which was made of sanded wood pockmarked with knife cuts of men's initials.

"Americano! Welcome!" the bartender said in English, sauntering up.

"That obvious, huh?" Ruben said in Spanish.

"That tourist hat's kind of a giveaway," he said. He leaned down so his eyes met Ruben's and smiled. "I'm Paco. This is my place."

"Ruben," he said, carefully removing his hat in a show of respect.

"What can I get you?" Paco said.

"How much tequila will this buy?" he asked, pointing to the bills.

Paco shrugged. "Depends. The locals drink mescal here. Kinda like rot gut tequila and takes getting used to. Seven pesos. Now if you want the good stuff," he said, leaning in close and lowering his voice, "and I'd highly recommend it, then it's twenty-five a shot."

"I'll take ten," Ruben said.

"You'll be drunk from five," Paco shot back, chuckling. "But you're the boss."

Paco scooped up the money and began pouring shots of blanco tequila from an unadorned bottle, stacking them on the bar in front of Ruben, along with a saltshaker and a glass of lime wedges. Then he folded his arms and waited.

Ruben stared at the salt and limes and tried to remember how men drank tequila in the movies.

Paco smiled. "You've not had tequila before?"

"No," he confessed. "But today's a real good time to start."

"Why's that?"

"The world turned to shit today," Ruben said.

"Sounds like woman trouble, hombre."

"Yeah," Ruben intoned. "You could say that." He ignored the salt and lime and took his first sip of tequila and instantly his face contorted. When the liquid slid down his throat, he was seized by a coughing fit. He glanced with his mouth agape at Paco as if to say, 'What have you done to me?'

The two men at the end of the bar, watching Ruben in silence, roared with laughter. One got up and sauntered over.

"You don't sip tequila, senor," he laughed. He scooped up one of Ruben's shots in his big hand and poured salt onto the webbing between the thumb and forefinger. "Like this," he said, downing the shot, licking the salt from his hand and then sucking the juice from a lime wedge. He patted Ruben on the back good naturedly and returned to his seat.

"That one's on you, hombre," Paco said to Ruben. "Try it again."

He did as he was shown, finishing his first shot with a backward tilt of his head.

"Better!" Ruben said through clenched teeth.

"Enjoy," Paco said, moving to refill the empty beer mugs of three of the huddled men, who sized up Ruben in silence and quickly rejoined their group.

Alone, Ruben redonned his hat, yearning to crawl inside it. Closing his eyes, he breathed in his surroundings; a Mexican radio station serenading, the musk of warm beer sloshed on a floor of concrete blotched in spots with silver paint. It was a darkish lair, lit mostly by neon beer signs and strings of miniature holiday lights taped along the floor's perimeter. He raised his eyes to the mirror, which Paco lit at each end with bathroom vanity bulbs. The soft hues made the liquor bottles show off their colors; browns, tans, reds and, with the mescals, milky whiteness like potions. Ruben was amazed booze could be so colorful.

He reached for another shot glass and swigged the liquor with the help of the lime. In minutes the alcohol, like a warm blanket, melted the tension from his arms and legs. He had another shot and then one more. His body burned inside from the heat; his mind welcomed the gentle fog.

Paco was back in front of him. "You're pretty quiet. Feel like talkin'?"

"You seem nice enough, Paco. But best leave me be."

"I can do that," the owner said. "Sometimes talking helps, though."

"It would just sound like a confession," Ruben said.

"I hear them all the time. Father Paco, they call me." He smiled and waited.

"I've done something . . . set some things in motion," Ruben said then. "It's too late for talk now."

"Suit yourself, hombre," Paco said as he strode away.

By the time Paco returned, Ruben was singing out loud to the radio, waving his fingers in the air, watching them blur. "Whoa there, Paco!" said Ruben. "Want a shot?"

Paco wordlessly downed one of Ruben's remaining drinks, shook some salt onto his tongue and was gone again to shoo a woman in a party dress who'd wandered in.

"Hooker," Paco said when he returned. "We don't do that here."

The bartender eyed the four shots remaining before Ruben. "You're not driving after this, right?"

"Nope. Got a room at . . . ahh . . ." He paused, searching his tangled mind for the hotel name and gave up. "Down the street."

"Okay, you're drunk. No more tequila for you," he said. Paco reached for the remaining shot glasses, but Ruben placed his hands above them.

"No," he said sternly. "Leave them."

Paco stepped backed. "As you wish," he said.

Ruben had another shot, then one more. The liquor was turning sour in his mouth and his head spun. He shook it off and used his hands to grasp the bar edge. For a few seconds, he thought he might reel off his stool.

A man in a sanitation department uniform was suddenly beside him, sidling up to the bar too close, glaring down at Ruben and drunkenly slamming his beer mug down, which spattered foam on Ruben's face. The man didn't notice, motioning to Paco for a refill with a nod.

Ruben wiped his face with his shirt sleeve, set his hat on the bar and rose from his stool.

"Couldn't leave me be, could ya," Ruben asked, scowling. Paco reached under the bar for the baseball bat he kept there just as Ruben connected with a right hook to the stocky man's chin that sent him to the floor.

Two of the man's friends were upon Ruben in seconds. They pinned his arms back, waiting for the heap on the floor to get up. Paco rounded the bar but the drunk rose and landed two quick punches to Ruben's face before the bartender wrapped the bat around his neck and pulled him away. Ruben crumpled to the floor.

"Pendejo," Paco hissed, standing over the unconscious Ruben. Gesturing to one of the two men at the bar, he said, "Juan, when he comes to I want you to help him back to his hotel down the street, the Ventura. Make sure he gets to his room. When you come back, those last two shots of his are yours."

Ruben had no memory of leaving the bar but awoke in his hotel bed. The afternoon sun streamed in like a frayed nerve. The taste of vomit on Ruben's lips followed him to the sink where he washed his mouth and chased a handful of aspirin with the remnants of a day-old Coke. The shower water was cold but roused him; he didn't shave his swollen face and barely combed his hair. Then he was out the door.

CHAPTER 21

2002 – DAY SEVEN

A package arrived at the Youngblood home. It was the size of a hat box, wrapped in brown paper and plastered with scotch tape, addressed to "Eddie Youngblood – For Your Eyes Only" in Ruben's handwriting. Only Ruben called his father Eddie. In the place where a return address would normally be was the word "Segovia."

"It's from Ruben," Gabby said excitedly as she hurried for her purse to pay the C.O.D. charge. "Edwin," she shouted down the hall, "there's a package here from Ruben."

Edwin shot out of his study, still dressed in his robe, and met the FedEx driver before Gabby had returned from the kitchen. He took the package and jiggled it in his hands. He trailed off toward the kitchen and scissors. Edwin dug around in the junk drawer till he poked the scissors tip and jerked his hand back. He noticed that Ruben had written "Eddie" on the label and smiled. These are the papers he'd mentioned, he thought. Perhaps some good news? He tore into the package, not waiting for

Gabby to return.

There was a note inside. It was brief.

"I've located my sister," it read. "It's quite a Revelation."

Edwin pondered Ruben's use of the name Segovia and the Biblical reference, which made him frown.

Inside the package, Edwin saw only crumpled up Mexican newspapers. He dug his hand inside, searching out the contents underneath. Suddenly, he shrieked in pain, just as Gabby walked into the kitchen. His hand flew up and he staggered backward, slinging the box to the floor. Two scorpions crawled out.

Gabby ran to her husband, who clawed at his hand. One of the scorpions had stabbed his stinger into his wrist. He looked down at the scorpions and knew they were of the variety he had seen often in Durango: the white scorpion.

Gabby lunged for a hard-bound Book of Mormon from the coffee table and crushed the scorpions with it; then called for an ambulance. As she spoke, Edwin moaned in agony. The pain was like none he'd known and spots began clouding his view like busy gnats. With the flat palm of his free hand, he felt about for the floor though still standing and then lowered himself to a knee. The gnats danced and multiplied as he lay flat on his back. His body spasmed slightly on the floor and drool trailed from his mouth. Gabby held his hand and prayed.

Across town, the arrival of a FedEx letter interrupted Rebecca's reading time with Megan. Inside was a note from Ruben, hand scrawled in jagged letters, saying: "Lord help us."

Attached was a copy of the missing person's report on Maria Segovia, along with a handwritten English translation. When she read about the birthmark, identical to her own, Rebecca fainted cold, striking her head hard against the wood floor in her den.

CHAPTER 22

Provo Police Lieutenant Luther Binion, on his knees with a hand-held magnifying glass, examined the flattened remains of the scorpions.

"Which of you pulled the trigger?" he asked softly, admiring the creatures' armor-like exteriors, pincers and stabbing stingers. "This is my first attempted murder by scorpion."

No one had heard. Binion slowly rose, hitched up his slacks and surveyed the activity in the Youngblood kitchen. Photos of the scorpions and the book used to squash them were complete. A crime scene investigator was at the kitchen island, pulling the contents from the FedEx package. He took photos of the box and newspapers used as stuffing and then handed three items to Binion.

One was Ruben Segovia's handwritten note to Edwin. Another was a two-page report of some kind in Spanish. The third was a page torn from a bible, from the Book of Revelation. Someone had circled verse 9, which said, in part:

"And the fifth angel blew his trumpet, and I saw a star fallen from heaven to earth and he was given the key to the shaft of the bottomless pit . . . and from the shaft rose smoke like the smoke of a great furnace and the sun and the air were darkened...Then from the smoke came locusts on the earth and they were given power like the power of scorpions of the earth..."

"Great," Binion muttered. "A passage from the Apocalypse. The press will eat it up.

"Get that report translated for me as soon as you can, Bill," the detective said. Through the front windows, he noticed a handful of people congregating along the sidewalk. "And keep the neighbors at bay out there, would ya?"

"Will do."

Binion, his silvery hair barely visible under an Italian fedora, sauntered toward the front door, admiring the ornate wainscoting of the colonial home, the classic lines of the mahogany railing along the stairs and the stylish antique furniture in the adjacent parlor area. Outside, he tipped his hat to the neighbors and made a beeline to his police sedan. He drove directly to Utah Valley Hospital, the city's largest.

Rebecca Youngblood came to with an oxygen mask covering her mouth in an ambulance enroute to the same hospital. She shook her head in groggy protest. Above her, an EMT was monitoring her vitals and when he saw her eyes trying to focus, he turned down the oxygen and told Rebecca where she was.

"You fell and hit your head," he said soothingly. "You've got a nasty bump there."

She tried to think. What had happened? And then it hit her: The text, the police report, the birth mark.

"Ruben's sister . . . is me!" she shrieked into the mask.

The attendant looked at the wide-eyed patient quizzically. "What?" he asked, raising her mask so she could speak.

"I married my brother! We had a child!" she said, her eyes ablaze. She searched the EMT's face for some sense of comprehension. "Don't you see? We're damned! The Church will abandon us. God will abandon us."

The EMT quickly secured the oxygen mask to her mouth again and prepared a sedative that he injected into her IV. He radioed the hospital and advised his patient was suffering from head trauma and speaking gibberish.

Edwin, barely conscious in the emergency room, twitched again and again. A gasp escaped Gabby lips with each twitch as though electricity was surging out of Edwin through his hand and into her. Her breathing was shallow, like his, her face ashen, like his.

Around them doctors and nurses took vitals after administering a generic scorpion anti-venom. Gabby told them the scorpion that stung Edwin was indigenous to Durango, Mexico, where the species was greatly feared. The bishop's vitals were of concern. His blood pressure was high, as was his heartrate. His breathing was shallow.

Gabby, in a summer dress she'd chosen that morning befitting the beauty of a cloudless sky, sobbed into a kerchief in the hallway, leaning against the white tiled wall. She started a silent prayer but was interrupted.

"Ma'am, I'm Detective Binion of the Provo Police Department. Are you Gabby Youngblood?" The stranger sidled beside her carrying a fedora in his large hands.

"Yes," she said. She eyed him politely but Binion saw panic in her eyes. Things were not going well. Her pupils were dilated and black. "Why are you here?" she queried.

"The ambulance crew notified us about the scorpion sting and the package that arrived this morning. At this point we're treating this as an attempted murder. Are you up for answering a question or two?"

Gabby shook her head in disbelief. "Fine," she said.

"You told the arriving officers that your son, Ruben Youngblood, was adopted and has a birth name of Segovia, correct?" Binion said. When she nodded, he continued. "And Ruben is in Mexico now, in Durango, which is where these white scorpions live?"

"Yes."

"But you said you have no idea why your son would do this?" he continued.

"No."

She faced the detective and looked him in the eye. "It has something to do with his missing sister, I think. But I don't know what."

Binion, a skilled listener, nodded patiently.

"When he met his biological mother, he learned he had a younger sister who was kidnapped as a baby," Gabby continued. "He told us he was trying to find her . . . but then he just went silent.

"And then we got this FedEx package," she said. Tears pooled in her eyes again.

"Okay," Binion said, "That's enough for now. Thank you, ma'am, for your time."

Binion placed a call to Rebecca Youngblood. Angeline Vega, who was at her daughter's house caring for Megan, answered the phone and advised Rebecca had been found unconscious by her daughter earlier that morning and rushed to the hospital.

Rebecca had been moved from the E.R. to intensive care by the time Binion located her. A series of scans to her head turned up nothing to suggest her injury was serious. She was asleep when the detective, hat in hand, ambled into the room. He introduced himself to Joe Vega.

"Do you know about the bishop?" he asked quietly.

Joe shook his head.

"Bishop Youngblood received a FedEx this morning containing two poisonous scorpions from Mexico. One of them stung him. The package was sent by your son-in-law," the detective said.

Joe's mouth gaped. "What?" he said.

Binion continued. "Do you have any idea why he might have wanted to kill his father?"

Joe's wide eyes stared blankly back at Binion. He shook his head vigorously. "No," he said meekly.

Binion took a chair beside Joe. "When did you speak to him last?"

Vega relayed his conversation from two days earlier.

"And Becky was indeed adopted like Ruben said she was, right?" the detective asked.

"Yes. We picked her up in El Paso twenty-three years ago," Joe Vega said. "Becky didn't know she was adopted. She didn't know anything about anything until Ruben called us."

The detective looked over at Rebecca. Her eyes appeared to be moving under her closed eyelids. He noticed also that her index finger attached to a blood oxygen monitor twitched every ten seconds or so. She would be coming around soon.

"One more thing," Binion said. "Did Bishop Youngblood play any role in your daughter's adoption?"

"No. He was back here in Provo when we got Becky," Joe said. "We did use the same adoption agency the Youngbloods used when they adopted Ruben. But that was the only connection."

Binion nodded. In a few moments, Rebecca was blinking herself back to consciousness. Her father's face came into focus.

"My head hurts," she said. She squinted her eyes to convey the pain.

"I'll see if we can get something," Joe said, and he pressed the attendant button at her bedside.

Detective Binion remained seated, out of Rebecca's immediate vision, and waited as a nurse stepped inside. Rebecca focused on him.

"Did you need something?" the nurse queried.

"My head hurts," Rebecca repeated.

"Of course. I'll be right back."

Binion stood then and ambled to Rebecca's bedside.

"Do I know you?" Rebecca asked.

"I'm Detective Luther Binion of the Provo Police Department," he said softly. "I'm afraid something terrible has happened and I need your help trying to understand it."

Rebecca was silent for a moment. Then she met Binion's eyes and said, "He's killed Edwin, hasn't he?"

"No. But he may have tried. How did you know?" the detective said.

"Got a FedEx this morning from Ruben." She closed her eyes and clinched her jaw in pain. "My head hurts."

Rebecca's father pressed the attendant button again just as the nurse returned with ibuprofen. Rebecca sucked them down. Noting that her heartrate and blood pressure had become elevated, the nurse decided to add a mild sedative to her IV. As it took effect, the tension in her face melted away.

Binion scanned the room and spotted the red and white FedEx letter that Angeline had found at Rebecca's house and given to Joe. He retrieved it and read Ruben's handwritten note and translation of the Durango police report. He reread it and frowned. Then he noticed a lump in the bottom of the cardboard envelope. There was something else inside. Binion reached his hand in and fished out a small vial containing a milky white liquid. There was no label on it but Binion knew instantly what it was.

"Excuse me," he said to Rebecca. "I'll be right back."

"What is it?" she asked.

"I'm pretty sure this is scorpion anti-venom from Durango. Your father-in-law desperately needs this now," he said as he hurriedly left the room. He returned minutes later.

"Your husband didn't really want to kill his father, Rebecca," Binion said as he sat back down beside her. "He wanted him to suffer, yes. But he wanted you to save him."

Rebecca looked at Binion incredulously. "I don't understand," she said.

"I think Ruben Youngblood is a very conflicted man,"

the detective said. "He's angry and lashing out. His life is upside down. But he's not the killing kind, I don't think."

Blip . . . blip . . . blip. The room was silent save for the cadence of the heart monitor.

Rebecca's eyes locked on Binion's. Finally, he spoke again. "Do you know someone with a birthmark that matches the one in this report?" he asked.

"Me," she said.

He sighed. "That would suggest you and your husband are half-brother and half-sister?"

"What else could it mean?" she said, looking at her father, who was ashen, his mouth obscenely open.

The detective frowned. "The odds of something like that happening would have to be a million to one," he said. "You two meet in college here?"

"Sort of. We were introduced through our parents," she said.

"Thousands of miles from where you both were born," he intoned. "Do you really think that's feasible?"

"I wish I knew," Rebecca said. "Ruben obviously thinks so."

Binion noticed the blips were going faster and Rebecca's face had gone crimson, despite the sedative.

"Rebecca, I think that's enough for now," he said gently, then ambled outside to the nurse's station. He ordered a DNA sample on Rebecca and drove to the police department downtown, where he wrote his report.

The next morning brought with it a chill wind that crept into Edwin's hospital room and woke him shivering.

The sweats he'd endured during the night were gone; his breathing normalized. He lapped at the tasteless hospital coffee, asked Gabby for another blanket, and stared at the breakfast in front of him.

The news of the day would carry a chill of its own. Gabby knew why Ruben had sent the scorpions after speaking to Rebecca and Joe Vega. And there were the dozens of frantic phone calls from friends, which she had ignored, and two from a reporter for the Provo Daily Herald.

She couldn't help but wonder what the world had awakened to. She excused herself and hurried downstairs to the gift shop.

"My God," Gabby said aloud as she stared at the newspaper.

"Incest revelation spawns assault on Mormon bishop, police say" the headline trumpeted across three columns of the front page.

"Read it to me," he said when she returned.

She sat down, unfolded it, and began. When finished, Gabby lowered the paper and began to cry. Edwin moved his hand to her leg to comfort her and closed his eyes.

"I've got to find my son before he kills somebody," he said finally.

CHAPTER 23

Ruben Youngblood eyed the rental car glovebox with annoyance. His pistol rattled inside it over potholes and cracks on the backroads leading back to Durango. There was one bullet in the chamber. He tried to imagine the slug, when the time came, going through his brain at day's end. It was meant for him. He hadn't loaded the gun when he accosted Red. It hadn't felt good in his hands from the beginning.

On top of his backpack on the passenger seat, the bagged scorpions clenched and unclenched their pincers with each jostle of the road. *You're built for this*, Ruben thought, eyeing them. Born killers. Always ready, sleeping in armor. He could not imagine better assassins.

The darkness was thick around him, pressing him into a seat back slick with sweat. He stunk like a moldy towel with stains ringing his T-shirt and shorts. Scratching at the stubble on his face, he lowered his hand to his neck, idly massaging it to relieve the tension and ache. He stuck his head out the open window to blow dry his oily hair.

In his short life, he'd never felt so utterly alone.

Durango was to the southwest, but Ruben's path

skirted the foothills of the Sierra Madre farther east where Teresa Cortez would be sleeping in her high-walled hacienda. He pulled his car over after midnight and slept in a parking lot until morning.

Lt. Binion, learning from Joe Vega that Ruben had contacted his wife about Maria's milk allergy, surmised Ruben had likely seen her adoption file. He immediately contacted El Paso police and alerted them to check on Sterling Pierce. He was told police got an anonymous call the day before and found Red, groggy but awake, still seated with his feet encased in a cardboard box.

He was rushed by ambulance to a local hospital. His diabetic right leg was blue.

Edwin rushed home and put in a call for Binion. "Lt. Binion's at the airport, I imagine," said the detective who answered.

"When's his flight?" Edwin asked.

"Ten I think."

Gabby drove him. At the terminal, Edwin found a Delta flight to Dallas-Fort Worth at 10:05 and bought a ticket with a connection to Durango. At the gate, he ducked behind a pillar, scanning the seats for a man in a fedora. He didn't get in line until the hatted man boarded. Passing him in the aisle, Edwin noticed his eyes were closed. But when he walked off the plane at DFW, Binion was waiting for him.

"You'll do everything I say," he said. "You'll stay in the car as long as I say. You'll keep out of my hair. Understood?"

"Understood," Edwin said.

In Durango, the detective rented a car and drove to the barrio of Rosa Segovia, where he swabbed her mouth for DNA, while Edwin waited outside. Durango police helped him locate addresses for Cortez and Marmoles.

Ruben parked a quarter mile from the Cortez compound and made his way on foot. Passing a stand of cactus, a rustling underneath startled him. A rattlesnake was contorting to swallow a smaller rattler for breakfast. It convulsed its scaly body to force its meal inside, inching its flexible jaws forward to fit it all. The scene made Ruben shiver. Turning away he trudged to a spot at a hill crest with a full view of the hacienda.

He lay in the warm sand, blocked the sun with his hand and squinted. He faced the front gate, a wrought-iron affair, black and twisting with the letter "C" molded into the center. Beyond it he could see a gardener in a wide sombrero tending to trees bulging with limes. The front door was mostly glass but he saw no movement beyond it.

When the sun was high, he reached in his backpack for his gun. When he withdrew it, there was a scorpion on his hand that struck in an instant. He shook it off, dropped the pistol and screamed, startling the gardener. Ruben raised himself up, kicked the scorpion away and stared at the sting mark on his right hand. It was red and swelling. With his left hand, he reopened his backpack and saw the other three scorpions were still inside the sandwich bag. He sealed it with his shaking fingers. The pain was blinding. He could feel his heart pounding. He dropped the gun in the backpack and walked toward the house, breathing hard. At the gate he felt his legs give way; he crumpled to the ground then felt himself being dragged.

"Are you Ruben?" a voice asked. "Can you hear me?"

The sound came from nowhere, like an echo. As light filtered through his eyelids, his senses detected a pillow under his head and the cool hardness of tile on his back. Blinking open his eyes, he was bombarded with blurry red, yellow, and orange light above him. The swatches of color eventually revealed themselves as cut glass attached to a ceiling light cover. He was in the hacienda's foyer, surrounded by scrubbed adobe walls of soft yellow.

Instinctively he tried to reach with his right hand for his backpack but saw that his hand was inside a bag filled with ice. The backpack wasn't there.

"Better lie still, Mr. Ruben Youngblood," said a second voice. "Be a shame if you die before the police get here."

On her knees beside him was a woman with a blurry face, eyeing him intently. But she wasn't the one who had spoken. The second voice, of a woman much older, came from behind him somewhere.

"What kind of scorpion stung you?" asked the voice.

"A white one." He strained his head to see her but could not. It was a raspy voice wrapped in thick congestion that made her cough and revealed a sickly rattle in her lungs. She spat phlegm into something and cleared her throat.

The younger woman rose and disappeared, just as the other voice materialized from the shadows, its physical form slowly inching a wheelchair into the foyer. The apparatus was well oiled and silent as she glided beside him until, using one thick arm as a brake and the other to pirouette, she was facing him, wearing orange hospital scrubs and thick white socks. Her hair was salt and pepper and clipped in back and she wore no makeup, betraying crevasse-like wrinkles on her brow and sagging jowls below her chin. A trace of spittle dangled from one side of her mouth.

She placed her hands across a midriff covered by a thin cotton blanket. Leaning forward slightly, she said, "You were wrong to send those scorpions to your father, Ruben. Clever choice of murder weapons but he didn't deserve that."

She scanned him for traces of recognition, having known him only briefly as a swaddled baby. In a few moments, she nodded as if she could see the baby in him still.

"He's not dead, you know," she added.

"Oh?" Ruben asked.

"Your little stunt made the papers, even in Mexico. Scorpions. Kidnapping. Incest. What a story!"

"What did it say about my father?"

"It said he was stung only once. He's fine by now I'm sure." As she stared at him, a scowl pursed her lips. "It appears, though, that you had a worse fate in mind for me." She reached under her blanket and, using two fingers, held out the sandwich bag retrieved from Ruben's backpack with the three scorpions inside. "These are for me, yes?"

Ruben glared back in silence.

The other woman was back beside him then, silently offering water. She had a smooth complexion befitting a life spent indoors and seemed riveted on his dirt-ringed face. He looked at her sheepishly and blinked.

"I'm not fond of scorpions," Teresa Cortez continued,

examining the bag's contents. She shook it and watched as they raised up on tiny legs and opened their pincers in defiance. "In fact, these are the first ones ever in this house. I took precautions when I built this place. I had them put sulfur in the soil before they laid the foundation. There's sulfur inside the concrete blocks as well. The wall around the house keeps the snakes and coyotes out. It's pretty much pest proof."

She dropped the sandwich bag to the floor and rolled atop it with her wheelchair. Back and forth, she crushed each creature.

"You're a different kind of pest." She leered disdainfully, then drew her kerchief to her mouth and coughed again. "Pablo, my gardener, dragged you in. I wouldn't have bothered.

"Gnats are best swatted."

"I'm Juanita," the woman beside him said in English.

Teresa shook her head in annoyance. "Child, go tell Pablo to bring his snake shooter in here."

Ruben, meanwhile, was listening to what his body was telling him. He had no idea how long he'd been unconscious but the heart pounding in his ears had ebbed and the cobwebs in his head were beginning to fall away.

He lunged for her then, hoping to capsize her wheelchair but she was prepared for it, drawing a pistol from under her blanket. She shoved the barrel against his forehead before he could rise out of his crouch.

"Stop!" she shouted. Her voice echoed off the walls of the high-ceilinged foyer. He had his hands on the arms of her wheelchair and glared at her defiantly. She cocked the pistol and waited, with lips pursed, until he let go and sat on his haunches. Pablo appeared a moment later with a sawed off .410 shotgun and pointed it at Ruben from behind.

She and Pablo escorted Ruben into the main room, where he sank deflated into a chair beside the couch. Juanita stood transfixed nearby.

"Juanita, why don't you fix some fresh lemonade. The police will be thirsty when they get here," Cortez said.

Behind her large windows framed a courtyard with a fountain cascading water tier by tier into a spacious pond surrounded by flowers of white and yellow, where misters attached to wood lattice that sliced the sun's rays into a checkerboard made the petals bob and dance with the weight of the droplets. To the left of the courtyard, picture windows bathed a separate dining room with sunlight. On the other side was the kitchen, where Ruben could see Juanita squeezing lemons by hand. The room they were in was long, with high ceilings bedecked in the middle by a huge, wrought iron chandelier with intricately cascading multi-colored glass shards. Long necked ceiling fans on either side cast sleepy shadows along the floor.

Cortez watched Ruben's eyes.

"Not bad for a lowly nurse, huh?" she asked.

"Kidnapping must have been lucrative." He scowled.

"That clinic of your father's drew expectant mothers like moths to flame but demand for babies in the States was bigger. So we expanded operations a bit."

"You admit to the kidnappings then?" he shot back.

"I admit to helping babies out of poverty," Cortez retorted. "Maria Segovia was one of those. I imagine she's grateful for it."

Ruben glared at her sunken eyes. "You really think you can sugarcoat baby stealing?" he said. "Did my father know?"

"I did this on the side. Red didn't even know. Your father? Clueless." The old woman took a breath but was overcome by a coughing fit. Her lungs rattled from the sticky mucus inside them. "Nobody cared where the babies came from. Nobody.

"I filled out the birth certificates as I pleased. No one questioned them," she said. "Until now, that is."

"You brought Maria Segovia into the world, yes?" Ruben queried.

"I most certainly did."

"Then you had her kidnapped and sold her off into adoption to friends of my family and I ended up married to her!" he said. "My own sister!!"

"Well, it wasn't quite like that, Ruben," she said, amused. "Not like that at all.

"Let me ask you something, pretty boy," she went on. "Anything about Juanita look familiar?"

"What are you getting at?" Ruben snapped.

"She's my daughter."

"I figured as much." He looked toward the kitchen and faintly heard Juanita humming to herself while cutting lemons. Her face, he thought, had a certain grace to it, so unlike her mother's.

"She's pretty, isn't she? Edwin thought she was pretty."

Ruben's head jerked up. "What?"

"She worked nights for me at the clinic for several months. Got to know your father pretty well, I'd say."

Ruben glared.

Teresa roared with laughter, raising her head and clattering her voice toward the ceiling. But just as quickly another coughing fit began; a wrenching one that made her gasp for air between tremors. She squeezed her knuckles white on the arm rests of the wheelchair.

Ruben seized the moment. He ripped off the bag covering his hand and flew out of his chair, startling Pablo, who squeezed the trigger on the shotgun, firing it harmlessly into the ceiling. As Teresa fumbled for her pistol, Ruben was upon her, wrestling for the gun. One round went off just past Ruben's face, burning his left cheek with hot gunpower as the bullet embedded in a wall.

Outside, two state police cars and an ambulance arrived at the estate's gates as the shots rang out. Lt. Luther Binion, who had intercepted the caravan at the base of the foothills, wheeled up behind and ordered Edwin to stay in the car. The troopers and Binion drew their pistols and took up positions behind the outer wall, while one officer dug a tear gas gun out of his trunk and called for backup. They were not expecting this. Teresa had told the state police dispatcher the intruder required an ambulance.

In the battle for the pistol, her wheelchair was upended and she and Ruben landed side by side on the hard terrazzo floor. She grunted and wheezed until Ruben seized control of the weapon, leaped to his feet, and glared down on her.

Suddenly Juanita was beside him. In her hand was Ruben's backpack. She reached inside and pulled out Ruben's pistol, then tossed the backpack to the floor. She eyed her helpless mother.

"Shoot him!" Teresa said through gritted teeth.

"I can't!" Juanita stammered. "It's Ruben!"

Ruben jerked his head toward Juanita. "What?" he

asked. "What?" He turned to Pablo, who was shaking with fear and suddenly bolted for the front door, startling the police officers outside. One of them, seeing the shotgun, shot Pablo in the shoulder.

Another trooper had reached the main room's picture windows, where he saw Ruben and Juanita standing over Cortez, each with a gun in their hand. Without hesitation he used the butt of the tear gas gun to shatter a window and fired a cannister inside. In seconds, the room was a billowing cloud, burning the trios' eyes and throats. The chemicals rose upward and then back down, hovering thickly above the floor, where Cortez was getting the worst of it. She was choking, unable to draw in a breath. She clawed at her throat. The chemicals constricted her lungs and her body fought against it by producing more mucus. She was drowning in it.

In the confusion another shot rang out.

Both pistols clattered to the floor. Grabbing his backpack and Juanita's arm, Ruben made for the courtyard door through the stinging fog. As they reached it, two officers in gas masks stepped inside the main room from the foyer and, finding Teresa, lifted her limp frame and took her to paramedics outside.

The courtyard misters were like a salve to Ruben and Juanita, bathing their faces and eyes. Their feverish coughing began to ease. When they peered back into the house, two officers were there, waiting by the door in gas masks with guns drawn.

Ruben bolted, scaling the courtyard lattice work to the Mexican tile roof, using his swollen right hand like a bear claw to pull himself up. When he disappeared from the officers' view on the backside of the pitch, they headed back inside and out the front door, which was partially blocked by the paramedics working frantically to revive Cortez. It was the break Ruben needed. He leaped from the roof to the outer wall and down into the desert sand, where the afternoon heat was baking the ground the color of bread crust below the scrub.

Breathing hard from constricted lungs, he wound his way to his car and gunned it onto the main road toward Durango, well ahead of the two troopers giving chase. Knowing his rent car was no match for a police cruiser, Ruben scanned the open road for a hiding place and, spotting a wide rain culvert, swerved beneath the overhang, and waited.

The troopers passed above at high speed and with his car engine idling, Ruben fought to calm his wheezing. His heart raced and head pounded. But his mind was fixed on Juanita.

Instead of Teresa dead on the floor, it should have been Ruben by Juanita's hand. She'd refused her mother's bidding. *But why?* he asked himself. She'd spoken as though she *knew* him. "It's Ruben," she had said. What did she mean? Was the resemblance more than a coincidence? Did she and Edwin have an affair?

Ruben put the car in gear and caught the first thoroughfare north to skirt around Durango, in the direction of the ranch of Eduard Marmoles. His mental compass was failing him now. But he pressed on.

At the Cortez compound, the paramedics discovered a gunshot wound in Teresa's chest. They loaded her in the ambulance beside Pablo and sped away.

Binion, with no jurisdiction in Mexico, volunteered to assist the remaining state trooper with cataloging the crime scene. They marked, photographed, and removed the .38 caliber slug from the wall and took a photo of the pellet holes in the ceiling. Binion tried to map the weapons' trajectories, using stick figures to reconstruct who was where when each gun was fired. They dusted the pistols for fingerprints, bagged each weapon and collected the dead scorpions. They photographed the wheelchair, laying on one side, drew a rough sketch of where Teresa Cortez was found and photographed the blood in the middle.

Juanita, whose lack of emotion about the condition of her mother was of keen interest to Binion, had disappeared into the kitchen, where the lawmen found her carefully washing her hands.

"Did you witness the shooting?" the detective said.

"I heard a gunshot and Ruben was standing right there, almost on top of her. But I couldn't see anything in the fog," she said. She used a dish towel to wipe her reddened eyes.

The trooper spoke up. "Speak in Spanish, please," he said. "One of the other officers said you were holding a gun next to Ruben."

"Yes, my mother told me to shoot him, but I couldn't," she said. "I dropped it on the floor. I guess Ruben picked it up."

"But he already had a gun," the officer said.

"I'm not sure what happened. I couldn't see."

"You won't mind if this officer tests your right hand for gunpowder residue, then?" Binion asked in English.

She nodded and repeated in Spanish what the detective had said, prompting the Mexican police officer to go in search of his crime scene kit.

"Oh my, where are my manners?" she said then,

smiling at Binion. "Would you like some lemonade?"

CHAPTER 24

Ruben fumbled with the gate code to the Marmoles ranch. Nineteen-sixty-two proved correct. He barreled along the dirt road to the crest that brought the hacienda into view. He didn't slow till he'd crossed the cattle guard and was at the high-walled gate overlooking the courtyard. The gate was unlocked. He peered through the front door at a darkened great room. Furniture was covered in fabric and plastic sheeting. The hall beyond it was dark.

He gaveled the door knocker three times. It echoed back faintly. He knocked again, this time pounding the door with his left fist. And in the back of the hall, a light blushed on.

Through the front door glass, Ruben saw movement in the hall; a moving shadow. Someone was coming.

He reached in his backpack for his gun. Gone.

Scorpions. Not there.

His fingers found the syringe. He grasped it in his hand and pulled the needle cover. He heard a dead bolt slide out of the way, then the click of a second lock. Ruben planted his feet firmly on the veranda plank wood, ready to lunge at Marmoles but as the door swung open, Ruben found himself confronting a smallish Mexican man in dirty cotton pants and a loosely hanging shirt.

This man could not be Marmoles, Ruben thought.

"Buenos Dias," the man said. And, also in Spanish, "Can I help you?"

Twenty minutes behind, Edwin and the detective found the Marmoles property gate open. Arriving at the hacienda, they discovered Ruben sitting in a lotus position atop the lawyer's grave inside the fenced wall behind the house. A simple stone marked the spot, where etched in granite were the words: Eugene Zimmerman, aka Eduard Marmoles, 1926 – 1997.

Ruben heard the soft crunch of their shoes on the newly mown grass. His eyes were closed and his arms rested meditatively on his legs. He didn't acknowledge them, presuming Mexican police officers were about to descend on him with guns drawn. The shoes stopped just behind him.

"Hello, son," the bishop said.

The young man's eyes shot open in surprise and his head spun around just as Detective Binion grabbed his arms, pinned them behind him and placed them in handcuffs.

"I'm Luther Binion of the Provo Police Department," he said coolly. "You're under arrest on charges of assault and attempted murder."

Ruben ignored the detective as he advised him of his rights. His eyes were fixed on his father and, without thinking, he began crawling toward him on his knees. His mental exhaustion loosed a wave of emotion; shame and guilt and doubt where before there had been only rage.

"Father, forgive me," he pleaded. Tears streamed down his tightly drawn cheeks.

Edwin, not expecting this, knelt and lifted Ruben's head so their eyes met. Like a priest, he sought to comfort but couldn't help reacting like a wounded father. "Yesterday you wanted me dead," he said. "Now this?"

"Over," Ruben mumbled. "It's over, Dad. You're not to blame. I am!" He leaned back on his haunches so that Edwin's hands fell to his sides. Ruben wiped his eyes on his sleeves.

"What does that mean?" Edwin asked, straining to understand.

But Ruben was silent. He seemed suddenly far away.

Binion stepped to the gravestone. "You talked to the caretaker?" he asked Ruben. "Ruben!" the detective repeated. "What happened to Marmoles?"

Ruben eyed the detective and queried, "Who are you again?"

"Binion. I'm a cop."

"Caretaker said rattlers got him a few years ago," said Ruben. "Somebody tipped over a terrarium with two diamondbacks in it while Marmoles was sleeping off a binge. Rumor was the cook did it after Marmoles raped her on the kitchen floor one night. Left behind an estate people are still fighting over, apparently. It's why the place just sits here in limbo. The caretaker, Pedro, said it's the best job he's ever had."

Looking on, Edwin barely recognized his young son. His clothes were sweat and dirt caked, his face was swollen and spotted like a leper's. He smelled like beer and piss. "What happened to your face?" he asked.

"Gunpowder burns. And a fist fight."

"And your hand?"

"Scorpion sting. Looks like yours did, I imagine," Ruben answered. He gazed into his father's eyes and saw glass bowls brimming over. Tears were welling there. "I didn't want to kill you. I just needed you to suffer."

"You accomplished that and then some," said Edwin, wiping at his eyes. "What did you learn from Teresa Cortez?"

"She admitted Rebecca is Rosa Segovia's daughter, that she was kidnapped at her bidding and then adopted out through your adoption network."

"So it's true. Becky is your half-sister. Oh, Jesus!" Edwin said.

Ruben shook his head. "I was right about Rebecca, but I was wrong about her being my sister. I'm pretty sure I'm not Rosa's son. My mother, I think, is someone else."

"Rebecca's not your sister?" Edwin asked.

"No," Ruben stammered. He hung his head with arms handcuffed behind him like a clipped-wing bird. "I don't think so. Hell, I don't know anything anymore."

Binion stepped between the two men and looked down at his prisoner. "I think I get it," he said. "I see a resemblance between you and Teresa's daughter, Juanita."

Without looking up, Ruben nodded.

"Since I was a boy, I believed Rosa was my biological mother. I wrote letters to her for years. I tried to picture her face and dreamt about what our reunion would be like," he said, and a hint of a smile formed. "When we met, in that pitiful hole she lives in, it was one of the most emotional moments of my life."

Ruben tried to stand but couldn't. Binion lifted him to his feet.

"When Teresa Cortez admitted she falsified Maria's birth certificate like it was nothing, I realized she could have done the same thing with mine. That possibility never occurred to me. Until today."

"Did Teresa say your birth certificate was fake?" Binion asked.

"No."

Did Juanita tell you she's your mother?"

"No. Didn't get a chance to confront her. You guys showed up."

"Well, there's still a lot you don't know," Binion chided.

The detective led Ruben to his car and placed him in the backseat. He retrieved Ruben's camera from his backpack and snapped photos of his still swollen hand. Then he swabbed Ruben's mouth with a DNA kit.

He turned to Edwin. "Follow me. I need an interpreter."

They walked to the front door and knocked. When Pedro answered, Edwin introduced Binion and asked if the detective could use the telephone. Binion, counseling Edwin to wait with Pedro, located the phone in the hall and when he returned, he announced he had contacted the state police and told them where to find Ruben.

"What?" stammered Edwin. "No! We have to get him out of Mexico."

"He's wanted for murder here. Teresa Cortez is dead. Your son can't run from that."

CHAPTER 25

Edwin watched helplessly as authorities uncuffed his son just long enough to put him in chains. There were four of them; four uniformed officers carefully shackling his arms and then his legs, which were connected by heavy links that rattled as he moved like loose hardware in a tool drawer. They stood on either side of him, led him to a waiting squad car, pushed his head down to door level and shoved him inside.

Edwin moved closer and saw his son grimace through the car window; the shackles were hurting him. Edwin placed his hand against the rear window and shouted in Spanish to the nearest officer "the chains are too tight!" but he was brushed aside wordlessly. Binion, stuffing his handcuffs back into their sheath on his gun belt, stepped up and led Edwin to his car.

"It's gonna be a long night for your son," he said. "With all the publicity, he's a prize. The good news is he'll get his own cell."

At the Durango city jail, Ruben was unshackled, stripped to his underwear, and placed in orange jail overalls. After his possessions were catalogued, he was marched to cell zero four, well below the city streets and lit solely by flickering fluorescent bulbs.

He bemoaned his plight for scant minutes before falling exhaustedly asleep.

Edwin was roused early the next morning by Binion, who pounded on his hotel room door.

"Turn on the radio," he said. "They're talking about Ruben."

Edwin found a talk radio station broadcasting a news conference: Durango state prosecutors were announcing that American Ruben Youngblood had confessed to killing Teresa Cortez in her home. State's attorney Ramon de la Hoya said the bullet found on the body came from the pistol Youngblood brought to her hacienda and Ruben had gunpowder residue on his face and hands. The state would be seeking a life prison sentence and de la Hoya described the murder as premeditated.

Edwin called the city jail and asked to see his son. He was advised only his attorney could visit.

"Get a good one," Binion advised. "The state's case is flimsy. Ruben didn't shoot Teresa. But a confession in a murder case will be hard to overcome."

Binion boarded a flight back to Provo. Edwin phoned Gabby and Rebecca and delivered the news that Ruben had confessed to a murder.

Ruben, on his bunk, watched beads of sweat drip from his forehead onto the concrete of his 6 X 10 cell. He listened to the ceiling vents in the hallway whoosh the stale early fall air. Occasionally he heard voices in adjacent cells. Cell doors clanked open and shut, faint sometimes as an echo, maddeningly loud at other times. His baggy jail scrubs were itchy and he yearned for a shower.

They had come to him in his sleep, adorning him in irons again and leading him to a smallish room with a solitary table and a harsh light that focused on him when he sat. A man in a button-down shirt, introduced as a prosecutor, paced the room while a uniformed police officer led the interrogation. They set into him hard, demanding he confess to shooting Teresa Cortez.

"Admit it and you can sleep," said the uniformed man.

"I didn't," he had said.

"Then who did?"

"Not me."

"You were standing over Cortez with a gun. An officer saw you," the interrogator said. "And you had motive. You wanted her dead."

"Juanita had a gun, too!" Ruben blurted.

The prosecutor stopped pacing and leaned across the table only inches from Ruben's face. "Are you suggesting Juanita Cortez shot her own mother?"

Ruben leaned back and closed his eyes. His dilemma was obvious. Was he to blame *his* mother for killing hers? Would anyone believe him if he did?

Reopening his eyes, his mind was made up.

"I shot her," he said, "It was me."

A stenographer was summoned who transcribed a brief confession that Ruben signed.

Awaking to a breakfast of huevos and tortillas slipped under his cell door on a metal plate the next morning, he swallowed the food like he had his confession, resigned to its bitter taste.

At half past one, a man with a briefcase in a tan summer suit was suddenly outside his cell, introducing himself as Arturo Torrence, a lawyer. "I've been hired by your father," he said, setting his briefcase on Ruben's bunk. "Which seems ironic since the newspapers say you tried to kill him two days ago."

"I don't need a lawyer," Ruben mumbled back.

"I can't think of anyone who needs one more," Arturo said. He took off his blazer and folded it over one arm. He paced a few steps, looking repeatedly at Ruben sitting motionless on the bed.

"Papers also said you broke into the home of a guy in El Paso who used to run adoptions for your father.

"And you went to the Cortez home with the intent of killing Teresa Cortez."

Ruben was silent.

"I'm pretty sure you need a lawyer. If not, then a shrink," Arturo said. "Which is it?"

Ruben stared at the floor.

"Alright. Here's what needs to happen. I'm your only contact with the outside world so the sooner you decide to talk to me the sooner I can see about getting you out of this mess."

"I signed a confession. I suggest you read it," Ruben said.

The attorney, perplexed, tried a different approach. "Perhaps you'd like to speak to your wife? If I could arrange it?"

"Can you do that?" Ruben asked, his eyes now on Mr. Torrence.

"Yes. A phone call could be arranged."

Ruben, feeling his eyes brim with tears, looked away. "What do you want to know."

"That confession you signed, were you coerced in any way?"

"No."

"Did they tell you what to say?"

"No."

"And did you force your way into the Cortez home with the intent to kill her?

"Not exactly," Ruben said. "I was carried in, unconscious."

"By whom?"

"The gardener, I think. a guy named Pablo. He got shot by the police."

The attorney began pacing again. He rubbed his goateed chin.

"There was a detective from Utah there, a guy named Binion. You confess anything to him?" Arturo asked.

"No," said Ruben.

"Okay, when you're arraigned, I'll speak for you and enter a plea of Not Guilty. It's important you do not contradict that in court. It buys us time to decide what kind of defense we want to put on. Okay?"

"I won't say anything," Ruben said.

"Alright. That's it for now," the attorney said. "Guard!"

Returning to his office, Arturo filed for a transcript of the call from the Cortez compound seeking police assistance on the day of the shooting. He filed a motion to interrogate the Cortez gardener recovering in the hospital. He requested access to the four boxes of adoption records found in Ruben's rental car. Then he contacted El Paso police and asked for a copy of the report on Red's ordeal.

Finally, he put in a call to Rebecca Youngblood in Provo.

CHAPTER 26

2002 – DAY ELEVEN

Rebecca heard the phone ring and began to cry. No more bad news, she told herself. Alone in pajamas in her childhood bed at her parents' home, she held her breath and waited for the ringing to stop. In a moment, Angeline Vega was at her door, gently knocking.

"Baby, Ruben's lawyer is calling from Durango. He wants to know if you'd like to talk to Ruben if he can arrange it sometime tomorrow."

"Yes" she said faintly and, raising her head toward the door and clearing her throat, repeated loudly, "Yes!"

"Okay, I'll let him know," Angeline said.

Rebecca rolled onto her stomach and cried into her pillow. Minutes later she was in the bathroom, blowing a sore nose. The cold she'd caught was sapping the last of her energy. In the mirror, she opened her mouth to scream at her reflection but could only muster a wheeze.

It felt better to cry. If she could just stop, she thought, she could go downstairs to cuddle with Megan. But she knew she'd melt in her arms and then they'd both be crying again, as had happened over and over the past two days.

Again, the phone was ringing, and Angeline was back at the door.

"Detective Binion has asked that you and Gabby come to the police station tomorrow morning at 9."

"No!" Rebecca blurted out. "I can't take more bad news."

"He said it's important."

"Will you come with me?" Rebecca asked, wiping her eyes.

"Of course."

The next morning, with her mother using one arm to prop her up, Rebecca, in a sweater and skirt, kept a handkerchief close to her nose as she wound her way down the long hall to the homicide division office. Once there, she couldn't remember who she'd come to see. Angelina chimed in.

"Binion's in the conference room," a civilian receptionist advised, pointing the way to a glass walled room with half open shades.

As they neared, the door swung open. Rebecca nodded at Binion and then saw Gabby already seated, dressed conservatively in a light wool dress accented with a white scarf. She made a beeline for her and they bear hugged while Angelina looked on disapprovingly.

"Why don't we take a seat over there," Angelina said, pointing at the far side of the table.

"I want to sit by Gabby," Rebecca said with some defiance. She pulled up a chair beside her and, once seated, held Gabby's hand. Angelina took a seat next to Rebecca.

Binion, in khakis and a dress shirt, with his longish

hair combed straight back, sat back down at the head of the table. In front of him was his fedora beside a stack of papers paper clipped in neat stacks.

"I took two DNA samples while I was in Mexico; one from Rosa Segovia and one from Ruben," Binion began. "They weren't a match. Rosa is not his mother."

"But the birth certificate . . .?" Rebecca stammered.

"The birth certificate was fake," the detective said. "He was right about you, though. Rosa *is* your mother. I took your DNA while you were in the hospital. You and Maria Segovia are one and the same."

Binion paused to let that sink in.

"Of course that firmly ties Edwin's adoption network to a kidnapping. You were sold to your unwitting parents through an El Paso adoption agency run by one of Edwin's elders, Sterling Pierce."

"Press is gonna make a meal out of that tidbit," he continued. "It's in the final report I'm releasing today.

"But that can't be," Gabby protested. "Edwin would never have stood for something like that."

"Edwin insists he played no role in any of that kidnapping business and there's no evidence to suggest he did," the detective said. "Your husband did some good things in Durango. A lot of people benefitted from those adoptions and not just the crooks who took advantage.

"That's gonna get lost in all this I imagine," he added, slowly rising from his chair. "And that's a real shame.

"We're done here, I think," he said. "I'm sure Edwin filled you in on Ruben's status in Mexico. The case against him here in Provo will go before a grand jury sometime this month."

Gabby hung her head and wept. Rebecca, still

squeezing her hand, struggled for words.

"Gabby, think about what the DNA evidence means. Ruben and I aren't brother and sister," she finally said.

Gabby acknowledged her words with her eyes and then nodded. Standing as one, they embraced again, both weeping over one another's shoulders.

Binion watched passively with hat in hand and then slowly walked out of the conference room and closed the door.

The next day's headline in the Provo Daily Herald was everything the detective predicted.

"Baby kidnapped then adopted through Mormon outreach in Mexico, police say," it said, with a subhead **"Former bishop's son confesses to murder."**

"We're ruined," said Gabby, putting down the paper. She padded upstairs in her robe and slippers. Minutes later she phoned an insurance broker to put their agency up for sale.

Attorney Torrence reached Binion from his car phone that afternoon.

"Lt. Binion, I understand you were there at the Cortez compound and you assisted in collecting evidence," said Arturo. "Would you be willing to testify if this thing goes to trial?"

"Yes, of course," the detective said.

"So what did you see?"

"I was outside the house when the shooting took place. But I can tell you what I think happened based on the evidence," he said.

"By all means," said attorney Torrence.

"The shooter was Juanita Cortez," Binion said. "Ruben's gun was used to shoot Teresa, but Ruben wasn't holding it. Check with the police dispatcher. She'll tell you Ruben was disarmed before he went into the house," he said.

"Already on it," said the attorney.

"That state trooper who tear gassed the place said he saw both Ruben and Juanita holding pistols. And the trajectory of the bullet fired from Teresa's gun shows that shot came from the floor, while Ruben wrestled for control of it. That's how his face was burned from the gunpowder residue. So he ended up with Teresa's gun. Juanita had Ruben's."

"She told me she dropped the gun in the confusion but if so, Ruben had to use his right hand to pick it up. His right hand was swelled pretty big. I don't think he could have fired a weapon with that hand," Binion said. "I took photos of it, by the way."

"Good," said Arturo. "So why is Ruben protecting Juanita?"

"I have an idea, but you'll need to get that from Ruben," said the detective. "Has he been cooperative?"

"Not very," the attorney responded. "Anything else?"

"Did you see the police report from El Paso?

"I did," said Arturo, laughing. "Imagine how surprised Mr. Pierce must have been when he learned there weren't any scorpions in that box after all."

Ruben, clean shaven and in a crisp jail overall, marched in leggings and cuffs two blocks to the state courthouse at eight the next morning, his attorney at his side. Four television crews and a phalanx of newspaper reporters and photographers marched beside them, peppering Ruben with questions about his motivation for wanting to kill Teresa Cortez. Arturo, who wore a tie for the occasion, answered "no comment" to all inquiries.

The arraignment was brief, a plea was entered, and Ruben shuffled slowly from the courtroom, casting a long glance at Edwin seated stiffly in the first row. The guards took Ruben to an empty witness room to meet with his lawyer. The attorney had requested the audience in the hope the press corps would thin out before the long march back to jail.

Ruben sat with his hands tucked between his knees. His face seemed tense to Arturo and he surmised the young man was shaken by the day's events.

"They're making a spectacle of you right now," he said, loosening his tie as he paced the room. "You're big news in Utah because of your father's ties to the adoption network. You're big news everywhere else because of that whole incest thing as a motive for murder.

"Do you still believe you married your sister?" Arturo asked.

"No."

The lawyer stopped pacing. "You believed it when you went to the Cortez compound. Now you don't?"

"That's right."

Outside the room the din of courtroom activity was increasing. Both men glanced toward the door as if expecting someone might enter and interrupt them.

"Do you believe in God, Mr. Torrence?" Ruben asked.

"Sure kid," he said, pacing again.

"I know there's a God. But my faith has been tested. When I thought I'd married my sister, something inside of me went dark. I wanted to hurt people I thought had hurt me." As he spoke, Ruben placed his hands on the table edge and listened to his chains rattling beneath his handcuffs.

"I don't want to hurt anyone anymore and that includes Juanita Cortez."

Arturo pulled up a chair beside Ruben.

"Juanita Cortez claims you shot her mother," the attorney said. "But you didn't, did you?"

"No."

"So you confessed to protect her," Arturo said. "That's what's going on here?"

Ruben slowly nodded.

"I know she was never a mother to me," he said. "But I've hurt enough people in my family already."

The attorney's eyes narrowed as he studied Ruben. He shrugged. "She's betrayed you already."

"And she'll answer for that before God," Ruben said.

That night, a Saturday, Ruben slept without dreaming.

CHAPTER 27

2002 - DAY THIRTEEN

"Game over!" Arturo shouted from his law office desk the first thing Monday morning. In his hand was a fax of the coroner's report.

Teresa Cortez died of asphyxiation, the coroner concluded. She was already dead when she was shot. The report said the small pool of blood found beneath the body and in her chest cavity indicated her heart had stopped beating before the bullet entered her chest. Her lungs were so fluid-filled that breathing wasn't possible. Conclusion: Death was through asphyxiation and deemed accidental, not by homicide.

Startled staff members buzzed around Arturo while he barked instructions. One scurried to draft a petition to be hand carried to the court for dismissal of the case. Another court filing demanded the immediate release of Ruben. Arturo himself rushed to the jail to deliver the news.

The presiding judge, Victor Castillo, called de la Hoya and Torrence to his chambers. Seated at his desk with an unlit cigar bulging his right cheek, he scowled at the counselors as de la Hoya made a move to sit down.

"Stand," the judge growled. "This isn't going to take long.

"Did anybody think to make sure that a crime actually took place before filing murder charges?" Castillo said, glaring at de la Hoya. "That's kinda like Law 101 isn't it?"

"Judge, she had a bullet in her chest, for Christ's sake," the prosecutor said. "And the defendant confessed to shooting her!"

"Well, he shot a corpse," said the judge. "And your case is dead on arrival."

De la Hoya winced at the sarcasm. "We're moving to refile for possession of an unlicensed weapon and perhaps assault," he said.

"Oh no you're not," said the judge. "I'm dismissing this case right now. Arturo, your motion is granted. Tell your client to get his butt out of Mexico."

"Thank you, your honor."

Arturo glanced at de la Hoya, whose face was scarlet, while the judge signed the dismissal. "Better luck next time, Ramon."

"Out," said the judge. "Both of you."

Ruben Youngblood stood at outtake in fresh clothes he was given from his backpack. Outside, a gaggle of reporters and cameramen waited. Edwin stood beside his rental car a half block away, ready to whisk his son away. Arturo had given Ruben instructions to keep his mouth shut so Ruben celebrated the moment with his fist, jabbing it at the sky outside the jail.

"I've booked us flights at noon," Edwin said when Ruben was in the car.

"We'll need to cancel them," said Ruben. "We have to

see Juanita."

"Why son?" Edwin asked, placing the shifter back into park and facing his son.

"I want to know why she shot her mother," he said, "and tried to frame me for it."

"Suit yourself," said Edwin. He eased into the traffic flow. His mind raced ahead of him, flashing back to the Juanita he had known, wrapped in a towel, then unwrapped and in his arms, lithe and warm with creamy skin and the faint scent of lilac water.

CHAPTER 28

Walking back from her mother's grave, Juanita washed her bare feet from a rain pail beside the porch of the Cortez hacienda, then closed her eyes and leaned back, letting the sun wash her skin in its warmth.

"Juanita!"

Her eyes shot open and she jerked her head toward the sound. It was Ruben, standing at the main gate beside an older man. He looked familiar.

Oh my God, she thought, it's Edwin!

She glanced about for a towel to dry her feet. Hastily she used the inside of her shift to do the job but grimaced at the pinkish wetness that bled through. She'd need to change again and thought of the blue dress in her closet. Setting her margarita down and rising modestly knowing their eyes were on her, Juanita put a smile on and walked leisurely to the gate as if expecting them all along.

Beyond the wrought iron barrier, Ruben smiled back at her, his hands half hidden in the pockets of his jeans. He seemed at ease to Juanita, in contrast to Edwin, who wrung his hands and shifted his weight from one leg to the other.

"You've got some gall coming here," she advised sternly.

"I was hoping to see you before we leave for Utah," Ruben said. "Could we come in?"

Juanita was silent. She eyed both men, curious of their motives. She wondered if either meant to do her harm but quickly discarded the notion.

"Why not?" she asked. Unlatching the gate, she slung it back and waved them through.

At the porch, she scooped up her margarita glass and walked briskly in. Ruben hesitated in the foyer, stopping to stare at the high ceiling he'd last seen in a haze from the floor, with Teresa Cortez's gravelly voice invading his ears while Juanita sought to comfort him.

Edwin passed him and entered the great room. Then he stopped cold.

On the floor near the center, crudely drawn in blue chalk, was the shape of a body. A bullet hole was circled in chalk on the wall nearby. Edwin turned to Ruben with his mouth open. They were standing in a crime scene: Ruben's crime scene.

Juanita spoke up. "I cleaned up the blood and the broken glass, but they wanted everything else left alone. Doesn't matter now. Excuse me while I go change."

Ruben glanced to his left at the picture window where the tear gas had come in, now patched with particle board. Looking up he saw the pattern of pellet holes in the ceiling and he could almost hear the sound of the shotgun blast again. He glanced to where Pablo had been standing that day and recalled the terror in his eyes. Fixating on the body outline he saw himself lunging at Teresa, toppling her wheelchair, wrestling away her gun as the upturned wheel spun slowly beside her. His hand instinctively brushed along his cheek as though the gunpowder from the pistol shot was burning him once again.

He shivered involuntarily.

Edwin, watching his son's eyes darting about, eased beside him.

"This is creepy," he said. "Could have been your body on that floor."

"I didn't care then," said Ruben reflectively. "I thought my life was over anyway."

Suddenly Juanita reappeared in her festive blue dress, pulling the skirt outward to either side, showing it off. Tiptoeing about in a pair of white sandals, she made no effort to hide her tipsiness.

"Do you like it? It's the latest thing in mourning attire."

Ruben and Edwin nodded uncomfortably.

She twirled like a ballerina and spilled some of her drink. "Whoops," she said, smiling.

"Stuck mother in the ground yesterday, in case you're wondering."

Ruben lowered his head, trying to feign a sense of reverence the moment seemed to warrant. "I, uh, I don't know what to say."

"She's food for the worms now," she said calmly before swigging down the remainder of her drink. "I was nothing to her but a cook and maid."

"Is that why you shot her?" Ruben asked.

"Ahh," she said. "You came to ask me that?" She plopped down on the couch and looked at Ruben impatiently.

"Well is it?" he replied.

"I shot her because she couldn't breathe," she said.

"She was suffering!"

"Why didn't you shoot me instead?" Ruben asked.

"You know why," she said indignantly.

"Because you're my mother?"

"Because," she began, pausing to leisurely readjust one of her sandals, "you're my son, yes."

Before he could respond, she quickly rose. "I'm thirsty. I have margaritas made."

"We don't drink," said Edwin.

"That's alright. I'm kind of new at it myself," she said. "Some limeade then."

She scurried into the kitchen. Ruben and Edwin took a seat on either side of the couch.

"She's half drunk," Edwin whispered. "We shouldn't stay much longer."

"I want to know more about her; maybe learn who my father is," Ruben whispered back.

The elder Youngblood's heart skipped a beat. "Does it matter?" he asked.

Ruben was silent. Something in his father's voice seemed odd. He probed his eyes.

"Is it you?" he said aloud.

Chapter 29

Juanita brought them each a cool drink, left and returned with a fresh margarita. She licked the rim and savored a long, slow sip.

Ruben barely noticed. His eyes were on his father.

"This is going to be an interesting day after all," Juanita mused, scanning the two men. "So, Ruben, you were going to ask me about the father?"

"I'm not sure I have to," he said with a disgusted shrug.

She smiled and set her drink down. "I was twenty-one when you were conceived, working for the bishop. He was a looker then and I made sure he looked at me, too. It was mother's idea I cozy up. She helped me pick out sexy jeans and a push-up bra," she said.

"I seduced him twice. I went to his bed, naked. No man could have resisted.

"Edwin was my first. But he wasn't the last," she continued. "One of the missionaries saw me sneak out of his room the second time. That afternoon, after mother went to work at the mission, that boy came knocking at our apartment. He told me what he'd seen and threatened to tell everyone."

"He wanted a taste to stay quiet, so I gave it to him. The next day, another one came 'round. He got a taste, too. When a third one came, I decided the secret was already out, so I ran him off.

"Turns out nobody had the nerve to talk anyway," she said. "I stayed on at the mission a while longer and on a couple of nights I serviced a few missionaries for money like the hookers used to do. Any of them could be your father."

Disgusted, Ruben stood up. He walked to the chalk marked floor and looked down, rigidly still. Edwin, with his eyes glued on Juanita, felt his face tighten into a sneer.

"What possessed you?" Edwin said between gritted teeth.

"I liked it," she said calmly. "I liked the physical contact. I needed the touching. I never got that from mother.

"Anyway, the hookers got wind of it and told her. That was the end of that."

Ruben, his face flushed, turned to face his father.

"Did you know about the missionaries?"

"No," Edwin said meekly.

"Why didn't you tell me about you and Juanita?" Ruben demanded.

"I'm not your biological father," Edwin said. "I can't have children."

"You should have *told* me!"

"I never told anyone," he responded. His face sagged with shame.

Juanita, assessing the impact of her salacious admissions, feigned indifference but couldn't shake a sense of amusement. There was neither love nor loathing there, for either of them.

Ruben turned his anger on Juanita. "Are you enjoying this?" he asked.

"I didn't ask you to come here," she answered sourly. "Either time."

She rose and walked to where Ruben stood. "But that confession you made. That was sweet. And stupid."

Ruben ignored the remark and continued to stare at the chalk mark on the floor. As Juanita's sandals appeared beside it, he noticed they were too big for her feet. He surmised they were her mother's and felt a twinge of sympathy that a woman of Juanita's age needed hand-me-downs to try and project an air of sophistication.

"You were kind to me," he recalled. "When we met."

She shook her head, choosing her next words, and absently chewed on her cheek wall with her teeth. The giddiness she'd been feeling was shifting to an inner melancholy and she took two deep breaths to collect herself. Exhaling a second time, she smiled politely at Ruben and took another sip of her drink.

"You Americans are a spoiled people. You live in big houses, drive big cars, think big thoughts. Everything's big, easy," she said. "Down here, people who dream big end up as crooks. The system keeps 'em down, so they break the rules. My mother became a crook. That's how she got this house built. Now it's mine. If you asked me to choose between you and this house, I choose this house.

"I wouldn't have been a good mother to you, son," she said. "It never occurred to me to try.

"Let's take a walk. There's something I'd like you both to see."

Outside, she steered them past Teresa's grave to the

back of the hacienda, where a 10 X 10 storage shed was suspended on concrete blocks. She jiggled a whittled-down spade handle from the eyelet where the door hinge met the facing and, after peeking inside for marauding insects, slung the door open. The late afternoon sun provided ample light and Ruben and Edwin peered in at four rows of shelves on three of the shed's walls. On each shelf were dozens of ash-colored oil lanterns, each with blown glass chimneys and metal bails connecting wooden handles that drooped off the shelf edges.

Ruben and Edwin were mesmerized. They looked like old railroad lamps conductors used to signal engineers through the steam. Edwin guessed fifty or more were there. They both turned to Juanita in wonder.

"My mother bought one of these each time she did an adoption through your mission, Bishop Youngblood," Juanita said.

Edwin's eyes widened in disbelief.

"She liked that slogan you had behind your desk about lives without purpose," she said.

"Lamps never lit," Edwin said, instantly remembering.

"This is ridiculous!" Ruben interjected. "Your mother cared about money. Nothing else. She kidnapped babies and sold them."

"I know," Juanita confessed. "I know what she did. But early on, before she got greedy and the money got so big, she believed in it.

"She cared about very few people, including me, but she *did* care about the babies." She looked at Edwin. "So, what do you say we put 'em up?"

"Up where?" Edwin asked.

"On the wall."

Ruben and Edwin eyed one another. If we leave now, Ruben was thinking, we might catch a flight to Dallas before nightfall.

But Edwin was intrigued. He grabbed two lanterns in each hand and Juanita lugged the kerosene can to the yard. "The ladder's over there," she said to Ruben, pointing between the house and shed.

They filled the lanterns, spaced them five feet apart along the perimeter wall and lit them, one by one. When finished, Edwin counted. Fifty-six. The sun was already on the western horizon and the lamps would soon be glowing.

"Wait a few minutes for the sun to set, then you can go," she said.

Edwin and Ruben followed her into the kitchen, where she fixed more lime-aid. Then she excused herself and when she returned, Ruben noticed she had a hard-bound book of some kind in her hand the size of a ledger. She set it wordlessly on a bookcase beside the foyer.

She joined them in the kitchen and they finished their drinks in silence. "I'll walk you out," she said.

At the front door, Juanita stepped in front of Ruben. He waited while she retrieved the ledger from the bookcase and placed it in his hands.

"She kept a record of the adoptions. I hope this brings you peace," she said.

CHAPTER 30

Edwin eased the rental car onto the main road descending from the foothills of the Sierra Madre toward Durango. Behind him in the rearview mirror the sun had given up its glow to the flames of fifty-six lanterns. They danced above the hacienda like upturned Mexican skirts in the crisp autumn air that made everything clear and sharp. He rolled his window down part way. It felt good, he thought, and he put his hand out and let the cool wind lift it gently as though it were a hawk's wing.

"So beautiful," Edwin marveled. "Like a ring of fire. Or a halo."

Ruben, who was busily flipping among the ledger pages, stopped to look behind him. The hacienda was bathed in yellow and orange light. Then he noticed Edwin, wearing a Cheshire cat smile.

"I'm glad you got to see the lamps lit," Ruben said, smiling back at his father. "You look like a kid with a snow globe."

"It has meaning for me," Edwin said.

"I know it does," said Ruben. He returned his attention to the ledger while his father drove on, peeking back often as the lights began to merge from fifty-six into one and then nothingness.

Edwin turned his attention to Ruben. "What's in the book?"

"Everything," Ruben said. "It's the nuts and bolts of every adoption. Who got paid and how much. It lists each mother – the real mothers – and who their babies went to. So much money changed hands. One adoption I saw went for $15,000.

"Here's one in mid-1976 for Baby Cookston, born Jesus Ramirez, son of Gloria Ramirez of Calle Guadalupe in Colonia Francisco, Durango," he said. "He was adopted by John and Cynthia Cookston of Salt Lake City through Heavenly Connections, Red's adoption agency. They paid $12,900 for Jesus. Red, Eduard Marmoles and Teresa got $8,500 of that. The mother got $500 and $2,000 went to a magistrate in Juarez, who must have signed off on the adoption. A bribe, pure and simple. There was $350 to Juanita for 'courier fees' and $300 for a "coyote" to get the baby across the border, it looks like. Then another $1,000 to LDS."

Ruben cast an eye toward his father. "LDS. Latter Day Saints. Your mission, dad. Did you receive money on some of these adoptions?

Edwin nodded. "On the ones that stayed in the dorm, yes. We were reimbursed $1,000 for our costs when they left. We had expenses, you know?"

"Course you did," said Ruben. "But on this ledger it just looks like a payout."

"It wasn't like that, Ruben," Edwin stammered. "We spent more than that just on food."

"I think," Ruben said, speaking slowly, "we shouldn't

share what's in here with anybody."

Edwin winced and drove on, toward the airport, where they found a motel. Ruben grabbed a pad of room stationery and began scribbling notes. Edwin flipped through the ledger, over pages containing names he recalled fondly, like the prostitutes the mission sheltered through pregnancy. He knew them by their street names: Randi, Rose, and Angel among others. In the ledger, they were simply producers of a commodity, entitled to their share of the proceeds. Edwin tried to visualize the handoff of merchandise; mothers passing their swaddled babies with one hand while Teresa Cortez placed a fat stack of pesos in their other.

Edwin excused himself to take a walk. The street in front of the hotel was congested so he wandered down a side street fronting a used car lot. In the middle of the lot was a single oak tree that seemed to be growing out of the pavement. He noticed strips of something white tied to its many branches. He crossed the street to the tree and read some. They each depicted a car sale. One said "1974 Mustang, Carla B, 19" and another "1955 Chevy, Jesus R, 64." They were each embroidered by hand on fine silk strips. Many were faded and frayed.

A salesman approached Edwin. "I saw you walk up," the man said. "You'll be needing a good car, yes?"

"No," Edwin said. "I just noticed this tree. Not used to seeing trees this big in the middle of a car lot."

"Car lot's been here going on twenty years. The tree came first at least forty years ago. The owner's wife sews one of these after every sale," the man said. "Too bad this old tree's getting cut down next month. Tree rot, from the inside."

Edwin noticed the leaves had thinned on the upper branches and many were yellowed. "Will the car lot stay?" he asked.

"Yes," he said. "But on hot days, I'll sure miss that shade."

Walking back to the motel, Edwin thought of his own legacy in Durango. He had heard the Church had ordered his portrait removed from the Bishop's Wall at the Mormon mission downtown. Edwin, like the tree, had become the rot, removed to preserve the Church.

When he reentered the motel room, Ruben spoke up.

"I found something," he said excitedly. "There were more than fifty-six adoptions. Seventy-two total. The others happened after you left. Among them each woman got $500 cash for giving up their baby.

"Except for eleven of them. And one of those was Rosa Segovia, Becky's mother. These eleven didn't get money because their babies were stolen!"

They huddled together and examined the entries.

"There are addresses here for most of them," Edwin noted.

"Are you thinking what I am?" asked Ruben.

"We should tell as many as we can what happened," said Edwin. "If nothing else, they'll know their children are okay."

Chapter 31

How bittersweet this tastes, Edwin thought, swallowing the day's dust and walking slowly up the still unpaved road beside the barrio casucha of Elisa Salvadore, where she had taken his hands into her own as he spoke of her kidnapped son being adopted to a family in Arizona. As he talked, she knelt and rested her head on his wrists; they were wet when he had finished.

"There are no words," she had said of knowing her son was alive. "My son is back in my heart. Thank you."

She rose unsteadily and embraced him. She felt quite thin to Edwin. Her teeth were ground down and yellow, her skin taut against her jutting chin. But a twinkle showed in her eyes.

Edwin asked if she intended to make contact.

"He does not know he was kidnapped, you say?" she asked. "Then I will not be the one to tell him."

Earlier that day, Ruben and Edwin brought four other women news of their children. Rosa Segovia's casucha was their last stop. Her door was partially open and she heard them approach.

"Ruben!" She was in her rainbow dress, newly

washed, and hugged him to her before they could enter, smushing the bag of groceries he'd bought from the mercado between them. She turned to Edwin and studied his face. "I have seen you somewhere," she said.

"I ran the mission where Teresa Cortez once worked," he said. "It was a long, long time ago. I'm Edwin, Ruben's adoptive father."

She spat on the ground after hearing Cortez's name. "What do you want?" she asked, eyeing him cautiously.

He asked to sit on one of her stools. She sat in the other. Ruben unloaded the food.

"I, uh, have news," Edwin began. "It turns out Ruben is not your real son. His birth certificate showing you as his mother was a fake."

Rosa turned to Ruben with an anguished look.

"It's true," Ruben said, flipping to the page in the ledger. "Your real son is Ruben Albritton of Oklahoma City. I checked on him. He's going to school at Harvard University, one of the best schools in America. He's doing great!"

"But how could this be?" she beseeched.

"The midwife Cortez did this," Edwin said. "She also paid someone to kidnap your daughter, Maria."

"I knew it!" She rummaged her mind to remember. "How do you know this?"

Ruben stepped beside Rosa and knelt, taking her hand in his.

"I went to see her and she admitted to it," he said. "I went to kill her. She died but it wasn't by my hand."

Rosa's eyes blazed. "Good! I'm glad of it."

"Maria was adopted by a couple in Utah," Ruben continued. "Friends of my parents. She is now my wife,

Rebecca. You met her. I know this is very confusing."

Rosa gaped at both men before homing in on Edwin.

"I remember," she said finally. "I met Cortez through your clinic. I trusted her because she worked at a church!" she said. "Your church."

She rose, raised her right hand, and slapped Edwin's face. She drew back her other hand to slap him again but stopped herself, scowling. Composing herself, she smoothed the folds of her dress and walked to the door.

"You let a scorpion in my house," she said. "Go from here!"

Edwin, his face still stinging, rose and with his eyes lowered walked silently outside.

Ruben followed. At the door, Rosa said, "Ruben, tell my Maria I will cook for her when she visits."

Edwin walked past his rental car and let his feet take him farther along the path, but it felt like going backward in time; to a flint-colored schoolhouse on the fringes of downtown Durango that once was a beacon of hope and purpose; a place that was part of a mission; of a people bent on good works.

The sting of Rosa's words echoed in his ears on the drive to the airport. "She was right. I *did* let a scorpion in," he said.

Ruben shrugged. "We've done all we could to set things right. Let's go home."

Rosa pulled a blanket from her trunk and, as was her habit before laying down, grabbed her broom for a quick sweeping, taking care in the corners to watch for the twitch of a scorpion's tail. Then she wrapped herself in the blanket and lay on her mat to sleep. Closing her eyes and listening to the ping on her sheet-metal roof, she welcomed the rain.

ACKNOWLEDGEMENTS

This book had its roots in a newspaper story that wasn't. More than thirty-five years ago, as a reporter for the *Fort Worth Star-Telegram*, I investigated reports of a shadowy "grey market" adoption ring operating out of Mexico that bought babies and sold them in the States. With the help of Spanish speaking reporter Frank Trejo, I chased leads from the "red light district" of Torreon to mountainous Monterrey but the code of silence that pervaded that underworld was deafening. It was a story I couldn't nail down. *Scorpion's Tail,* while pure fiction, was in a small way an effort to write about what may have been.

I wish to thank the unlucky souls who wrung their hands at my clumsy early drafts, including Author Jerry Flemmons (deceased), my best man Dan Malone (feisty as ever), Tom Korosec, my ex-wife Liz, Rebecca McDonald, and Sean O'Connor. All urged me on in his or her own special way, with insight and patience. A special thanks to Ken Dilanian for his candor and spot-on suggestions.

To the talented editors who turned this effort into a finished manuscript, including freelance editor Susan Strecker, you have my deepest appreciation.

About Atmosphere Press

Atmosphere Press is an independent, full-service publisher for excellent books in all genres and for all audiences. Learn more about what we do at atmospherepress.com.

We encourage you to check out some of Atmosphere's latest releases, which are available at Amazon.com and via order from your local bookstore:

Saints and Martyrs, a novel by Aaron Roe

The Recoleta Stories, by Bryon Esmond Butler

Voodoo Hideaway, a novel by Vance Cariaga

The Weed Lady, a novel by Shea R. Embry

A Book of Life, a novel by David Ellis

It Was Called a Home, a novel by Brian Nisun

Grace, a novel by Nancy Allen

Shifted, a novel by KristaLyn A. Vetovich

Because the Sky is a Thousand Soft Hurts, stories by Elizabeth Kirschner

Stronghold, a novel by Kesha Bakunin

Unwinding the Serpent, a novel by Robert Paul Blumenstein

All or Nothing, a novel by Miriam Malach

About the Author

A native Texan, G. Stan Jones spent his youth in the West Texas oil patch, served in the Navy and became an accomplished reporter and editor for the *Fort Worth Star-Telegram*. When the heyday of newspapers faded he chose a second career as a small business owner but never lost his itch to write. He now makes his home in Austin.

CPSIA information can be obtained
at www.ICGtesting.com
Printed in the USA
LVHW030507210521
688044LV00008B/500